Club Sixxes

ANOTHER SWEET SMILE

WENDI ZWADUK

ENTWINED PUBLISHING

ANOTHER SWEET SMILE

Dedication

For the Lucky Ducks
For KC
For TPZ
For JPZ

Chapter One

"Somebody come play with me," Onyx Power sang as she stopped at the bar and filled her tray. She sang along with the music on the speaker and paid little attention to the people who'd arrived at the club for the night. She'd come to Sixxes to scene and enjoy her evening, but like too many nights, she'd been roped into working. How could she say no? She owed too many people favors.

God.

"Are you here for the evening?" Sadie asked. She stood next to Onyx and filled her tray with glasses. "I wasn't going to, but they asked and I could use the tips."

Nice. Sadie got tips, while she had to work off debts.

"I am." She poured cola into two of the glasses, then lemon-lime soda into three others before mixing up cherry soda for the remainder. The club encouraged the attendees to drink, but nothing hard. Everyone was subjected to a code of conduct. No drugs, no booze and no illicit acts. If it was illegal or could impair the players without consent, then it was forbidden. She didn't mind. She'd rather everyone have a cool head than be silly drunk or worse. "I wanted to play tonight, but I don't know who I want. It's hard to figure it out. Who will be the right Dom? You know?" She had an idea, but it wasn't the right time to tell anyone she had a preference.

"I do." Sadie finished filling her tray. "There are some high-rollers here tonight. I heard there's a couple pairs of billionaires in the house. Can you imagine? Being snapped up by a billionaire? I'd so make them cover me in furs, diamonds and spoil me rotten. I deserve it."

She snorted. Of course Sadie would think she deserved to be spoiled. Sadie wanted everyone to bow to her and see her importance. She might be a sub, but Sadie had a wide dominant streak. If she wanted something, Sadie didn't stop until she got it, so everyone else needed to get out of the way.

Onyx wished she could be so forceful, but she didn't have it in her. Not after what she'd been through. "I need to deliver these drinks."

"You could be delivering to a man dripping with money. Keep that in mind." Sadie elbowed her. "You've got the slave garb on. Did you get a Dom? Or did you finally get a position as a club slave?"

"I just told you I didn't have a Dom, but I'm a club slave." She'd opted—not totally of her own volition— to be in service of the club and the Doms there for the evening. At any moment, she could be asked to join a scene and that thrilled her, despite her frustration with her position in life.

"Oh. I guess I missed that." Sadie shrugged then walked away, leaving her at the bar.

Onyx ensured the tray was clean and that she'd stocked it with napkins, then turned on her heel.

Walking around the club in nothing but the collar, cuffs, stockings, garter and heels pleased her. Her breasts swayed and her nipples beaded. A pair of clips with bells would be fun, but only if a Dom presented them to her. She liked being on display. Liked knowing anyone in the club could see her and might even be lusting after her. Might want to play.

For all she knew, her dream man could be there tonight.

She delivered her drinks to the various players, then carried the tray back to the bar. The chilly air swept across her body and her nipples beaded anew. She bit back a moan. She longed to be touched by a lover and Dom, not just the wind. To feel his hands along her ass, spanking her, bringing her pain and pleasure, his fingers swiping across her pussy, smearing her cream over her body and pushing into her with his hot cock.

One day.

"Are you interested in joining a scene?"

She stiffened at the sound of the man's voice. She'd heard this voice before, but never directed at her. She'd dreamed and fantasized about that voice. Part of her barely believed he'd approached her.

Zephyr Anderson. He and his business partner Jinx Collins were two of the richest men in the tri-county area and, according to the gossip sites, they were single. If one of them wanted to talk to her, then she'd pay attention — even if she hardly believed it was true.

She held onto the tray. "Do you need to me to take your drink order?" She smiled and met his gaze. Her hands shook and she gripped the tray. "What would you like?" She must've misheard his question because he couldn't possibly want her to play with them. Maybe he wanted her to perform for him.

That had to be it.

He tipped his head. "I didn't ask for a drink. I asked if you wanted to join a scene."

"Oh." She should put the tray down, but she kept it to hide the trembling in her hands. He'd not only paid her attention, but was asking her for one of her fantasies come to life. She should comply, but she should also answer him. Why weren't her legs working and where were her words?

"Do you want to?" he asked. "Girl?"

She didn't have the option to say no, not really. She was a house slave and had to cooperate with the Doms. But he was asking her if she wanted to play. Not demanding. Not pressuring. Nothing like any other Dom in the building.

She stared at him. Zephyr Anderson. All six-foot-five inches of him towered over her, even at her own five-foot-nine. He always seemed to have bed head, but it worked for him. Tattoos covered his arms and his brown eyes sparkled. She swore a stiff breeze would knock him over. She longed to run her fingers through his hair and hear him say her name. The gravelly sound of his voice always sent shivers down her spine. Was he tattooed all over? Pierced? She wanted to find out. She wanted to kiss him, too. Taste him. Kneel before him and have him pull her hair. She wondered what it'd feel like to have him fuck her. To hear him talk dirty to her and make her beg on her knees.

It'd probably feel like heaven.

What would it feel like to be between him and Jinx? She couldn't even fathom it.

"Girl?" Zephyr took the tray from her. "Do I need to turn you over my knee?"

God, that would be wonderful.

"Well?" Zephyr placed the tray on the closest table. "I can tell you're thinking about it. Maybe you'd like to discuss this in another room? Away from the eyes on you, and the listening ears?"

"I..." At least she'd found her voice. "I'm sorry."

"You're not interested?" He half-smiled. "I understand. It's a lot to be part of a scene when you don't know the players. It's fine."

"No." *Good God.* She massaged her temple. She'd fucked this all up. "I'm sorry." Her cuffs rattled and she pressed her lips together. She was there to serve him, yet she couldn't manage the words, *yes I want to play.* She had to look like a fool.

"Okay. I get it now." He grasped her hand. "Let's go into the other room. We need to talk and I want you to feel a little more at ease. There's a lot of pressure out here and this needs some discussion."

"Sure." She didn't fight him as he led her from the room. She probably should've been on a leash, but whatever. No one had signed a contract with her or collared her. For the evening and so many others, she was property of the club.

Except now she could be *his* property. What a delicious thought.

She straightened her spine and bowed her head. If he wanted her, then she'd do what he wanted. "Yes, Sir."

"So you can talk?" He opened one of the velvet-covered doors and led her into the adjacent room. "Good to hear your voice."

She's spoken to him already, but she understood his frustration. "Sorry, Sir." She should explain, when the time was right.

"Are you?" He let go of her and folded his arms. "I've seen you around the club. You're collared, but you're not someone's girl, are you?"

"No." She focused on the carpet. She wasn't supposed to look at him, but damn it, she wanted to. "I'm a club slave."

"I see. Just a moment." Zephyr walked away from her, then opened the door.

To bring in the boss? To have her punished, not in a scene, but for misconduct and non-compliance?

Fuck.

Another man entered the room and she fought the urge to look up at him.

Jinx?

God, she could only dream.

"You got her to come in?"

She pressed her knees together. She knew that voice, too. Jinx was there and discussing her. Holy shit. He was real.

"I did." Zephyr walked around her. "I think it's time we had a discussion, but that's only possible if we're all equals. What do you think?"

"I agree." Jinx curled his fingers under her chin, forcing her to look at him. "What do you think?"

They wanted her opinion? They were treating her like she had a stake in this? She cleared her voice. "I'd like that, if that's what you're offering."

"It is." Jinx caressed her chin, then let go and gestured to the sofa. "Sit."

She hesitated a moment, then settled on the cushion. She kept her spine straight and rested her hands on her knees. Was she on display? If so, then she'd do her best to make them happy.

Jinx dragged a wooden chair over to the sofa and faced her. He turned the chair around and sat across from her.

Zephyr sat beside her on the sofa. "As I said, we've seen you around the club and noticed you're collared by the club, but you're not collared by a Dom. Why is that?"

"I've never been asked." Never been approached for more than a scene here and there, or group play. "I guess I'm not what they're looking for." Not when the Doms found out why she'd been put into service at the club. They didn't want that kind of baggage.

"Why's that?" Jinx rested his arms on the back of the chair.

She forgot about the question and practically drooled over him. He looked every bit a model. He wore his jet-black hair short, almost in a crew cut. He smelled good and smiled easily. Where Zephyr was tall and lanky, Jinx was compact and muscular. He had tattoos all over his arms as well, but he had an air of sophistication about him.

"Girl?" The corners of Jinx's mouth curled in a smile. "What are you thinking?"

She'd been drawn to both men, but never had the gumption to speak to them. This was the time to speak up. "I'm too tall, too thin and I'm not a spunky, cute little sub. I guess they don't want someone who's me." Someone without her baggage or issues. She owed the wrong people too much and it'd be a long time before she paid her debt.

"I see." Zephyr crooked his brow. "I've seen you serving here. You're desperate to play and to be seen, but no one sees you. You help so they'll want you."

He'd read her so well, yet knew nothing. "Yes."

"And you're dying to belong to someone." Zephyr toyed with the shoelaces of his boot. "If you're going to be in a scene with someone like us, what do you like in your scenes? In your play?"

She'd never been asked this way—so plainly—but she had to respond. "I prefer discussion and debate to start."

"During a scene?" Jinx rocked back in his seat, then leaned forward again. "Very well. What are your kinks?"

Was she being interviewed? For a prospective position with them? She had nothing to lose. "I like spanking, toy play, cuffs, exhibition, blindfolds and I like orgasming, but I don't want penetration from just anyone until I'm fully collared. It probably sounds old-fashioned or ridiculous, but that's what I want. I don't want penetration if it's only for the scene. If I'm going to be penetrated, other than with toys, it should be because the Dom respects me and is only with me. I'm not afraid of going without a condom, but only with my Dom and with my okay." She'd been used a few times and wasn't about to do that again. She hated being a toy, unless that's what was expected from the scene.

She bit back the shudder and fought to bury the memories of that relationship. The past was something she'd rather forget.

"I see," Jinx said. "I respect your honesty."

"I also don't want a bunch of other players, unless you're requesting a voyeurism scene," she said. She realized how the balance of power worked here. She wore nothing, save for the slave uniform, but still. She wasn't about to be pushed around, unless it was in a scene.

"Very well." Zephyr nodded, then scooted closer. "We'd like to have a scene with you, just the two of us, using your kinks. I must ask, though, what you don't want."

"Yes, Sir." She folded her hands on her lap. "I should probably be on the floor for this. At your feet?"

"No." Zephyr shook his head. "This isn't the scene, yet. When we do, then we'll discuss what will happen."

Yet. When. The words gave her hope. "I don't get into blood play, knives, needles, gun play, kidnap play, suffocation or breath play. I don't want denigration or whipping. I'd prefer no extra partners in the scene and I don't want my own sub."

"Very well," Zephyr said. "What's your safe word?"

"Pumpkin." It was a silly word, but one not used in scenes. She flattened her hands on her lap. "What should I call you in a scene?"

Zephyr dipped his head once, then slid his gaze to Jinx before smiling. "When we play, you will address us both as Sir."

His tone gave her more hope. "Yes, Sir."

"Very well." Jinx nodded to the floor. "Would you like to play, girl? Tell us your safe word once more."

She sucked in a ragged breath. Holy hell, she did want to play. "I would like to, yes, Sir. My safe word is pumpkin, but I don't want to use it."

"On your knees." Zephyr stood. He widened his stance and folded his arms. "You know what to do, girl."

She did. She slid to the floor, then rested on her knees. She bowed her head before clasping her hands together behind her back. If she was ever ready to play, it was now.

She blew out a ragged breath as Zephyr, then Jinx, walked around her. She stuck her chest out to entice them. Not even an hour ago, she hadn't thought she'd be playing tonight. Half an hour ago, she'd sworn Jinx and Zephyr wouldn't want to scene with her.

Now both were about to happen.

"You've got beautiful breasts," Jinx said. "Just right for my hands." He knelt in front of her and slipped his fingers along one of her tits. He caressed her nipple, rolling and tugging on the tender flesh.

The move ripped a groan from her chest. She loved the pain of a scene. The sting delighted her. She spread her knees and the tingle in her pussy stretched through her body. Could they see her cream?

"These need clips. Next time, we're putting something on these to keep them nice and hard." Jinx palmed her other breast, then swatted it. "Like that?"

She trembled with joy. "Yes, Sir. Thank you, Sir. May I have another?"

"Not yet." Jinx stood, then stepped back.

Zephyr slipped his fingers into her hair, then tugged her head back. Not yanking, but gentle pushing and forcing her to look at him. She parted her lips. Did he want her mouth open? Want her to prepare to give him oral sex? She'd said no penetration, but if they used a toy or treated her with respect, she'd comply.

"You've got beautiful eyes, too." Zephyr leaned over and massaged her scalp. "Stand." He let go of her hair.

She did as he asked and managed to scramble to her feet.

"You like to be spanked?" Zephyr asked.

"I do." She shivered. Would he spank her? "Thank you, Sir. I deserve that punishment." Oh, boy, did she deserve that punishment.

"Then come here." Jinx clipped a leash onto the D-ring on her collar and led her across the room to the St. Andrew's cross. "You know what to do."

She did. She stepped onto the platform and spread her arms. She kept her back to them and bared her ass. A fresh wave of tingles shot through her. She widened her stance. Her skin prickled. Being put on display like this thrilled her. She flexed her toes in her shoes and wished she could press her knees together. If they swiped their fingers across her pussy lips, they'd find out just how much she wanted this.

Wanted them.

Zephyr strode around to the back of the cross and slapped a riding crop on the palm of his hand. "Do you want this?"

"I do, Sir. Thank you, Sir." She flattened her hands on the wood as Jinx clipped the cuffs to the thick rings at the ends of the cross. "May I have a spanking, Sir?"

Jinx trailed his fingers down her spine, then flattened his palm on her ass. The sound echoed in the room and the pain radiated through her body. She moaned, then arched toward another spanking.

"So needy." Zephyr twirled the crop in his fingers. "I believe our girl is ready for us."

Ready was an understatement.

"Tell us your name, girl," Zephyr said. "We need to know who we're playing with."

She fought the urge to use her fake name, Ruby. Why lie when she could be bare and honest? "Onyx."

She wobbled and held onto the cross. The worries in her mind, her concerns and anything else bothering her completely evaporated from her thoughts. They wanted her and they'd get what they wanted.

She'd make them happy.

Chapter Two

Jinx admired the view. He liked what he saw—he had since the moment he'd laid eyes on her. Onyx wasn't just beautiful. She was strong and sassy, but something about her tugged at his heart. He noted the bit of sadness in her eyes. She reminded him of a caged bird. She longed to fly, to sing her song and be cherished, he supposed. But working at the club had to be reining that in.

He wanted to make her happy.

Once he and Zeph had realized she wasn't collared, they'd decided to make a play for her.

Three days ago, he and his business partner, Zephyr, had come back to Sixxes after a month-long vacation from the club. As soon as he'd seen Onyx, he'd wanted her.

But that was his prerogative. If he wanted something—a job, money, material items, sex, a woman—he stopped at nothing to land it.

He didn't know her story, but he and Zeph had decided she was worth the trouble. The best things in life were never easy to obtain, always required an investment of hard work, and were totally worth the effort.

He admired the strength she possessed. It couldn't be that easy to walk around the club, collared but unclaimed, serving the players and remaining good-natured. She had to have confidence, even if it was unmined, to do the job. That or she projected well.

He didn't care.

Jinx moved to the back of the cross to face her. He trailed his fingers along her cheek and met her gaze. "Hi."

"Hi, Sir." She didn't smile, but delight filled her eyes. She parted her lips. When Zeph brought the crop down on her ass, she whimpered.

"Count them," Jinx said. "How many?" He continued to caress her cheek. The more he touched her, the more he needed to keep doing so. He brushed her hair from her face.

"One, Sir." Onyx trembled. Not from fear, but from excitement. "Thank you, Sir. May I have another?"

"Look at me." Jinx leveled his gaze. "Focus on me."

She gave a slight nod and did as she was told.

Zephyr spanked her four times, then twirled the crop before tucking it under his arm. "Girl?"

"Two, three, four, five," she said and groaned. "Thank you, Sirs. May I have another?"

"You may, naughty girl." Zephyr rounded her and handed the crop to Jinx. After he did, he withdrew a blindfold from his pocket. "Do you want this?"

She whimpered again. "Yes, Sir. May I, Sir? Please?"

"You may." Zeph slid the blindfold over her head and obscured her vision.

Jinx smiled to himself. She made a great kink model. With her long legs, slim body and readiness to perform, she made his heart happy. Not only that, but she had a good spirit. He hadn't seen the contents of her soul, but he knew. Anyone who worked this hard in a tough situation had to have a heart of gold.

He strode to the position behind her. A blush had already risen on her ass. He caressed the reddened skin. "How pretty. Do you like being marked?"

She sighed. "Yes, Sir. I like to please you."

She'd been trained well, but he wanted honesty. "Do you?"

"Yes, Sir. Thank you, Sir." She flexed her hands in the cuffs. "More, Sir, please?"

"In a minute." He left her long enough to select a vibrator from the rack. He slid a condom over the end of the toy. The next time they played, he'd have her do this work, but he didn't want to waste precious seconds right now.

Then again, next time they played he'd make sure she belonged to them. He'd sink into her sweet body to make her scream. Fill her cunt while Zephyr pumped her ass. The next time they'd switch. As long as everyone got off, he'd be happy.

He switched on the vibrator and trailed the end along her back. "Yes?"

"Yes, Sir." She moaned. "More, please, Sir? May I have another?"

She fumbled with her words and the struggle made Jinx happy. Not because he'd gotten her to crack, but because he'd nudged her to drop the practiced façade. He wanted the true woman. He reached around her and rubbed the vibrator on her tits.

She groaned and backed into him. "Oh, God."

"Do you like it?" he murmured against her ear. He loved the way she felt against his body. She fit along his chest and he longed to wrap her in his arms as he kissed her.

He and Zephyr had agreed they wouldn't kiss her on the first night. He knew why — any kissing led to attachment. They weren't supposed to get attached to her this fast.

Too late.

His heart wanted her. It was wholly an instant connection and she might not feel it yet, but he was hooked.

He stood behind her and slid the vibrator between her legs. He pressed the toy to her clit, thrilled when she jerked. "Like that?"

She whimpered again and bucked into him. When she moved backward, she mashed herself into the growing bulge in his jeans.

Every brush and bump into him sent his blood pumping faster. His cock throbbed against his zipper. *Shit.* He'd never be able to hold back this way. Not like this.

Zephyr snapped his fingers.

Jinx stopped vibing her and stepped back. He knew why — Zeph understood the attachments were forming. If they weren't careful, they'd bend her over and fuck her right now.

She whimpered and her head lolled on her shoulders. "Thank you, Sirs. May I have my orgasm?"

Jinx turned the vibrator off. He needed to put his hands on her again. To hold her. To breathe her in.

Instead, he gave the situation space. He waited for Zephyr to give them instruction.

Zeph nodded. The signal reminded Jinx to unhook the cuffs. Jinx unlocked the hooks, then helped her from the platform.

Zephyr winked. "Enjoying yourself?"

"Yes, Sir." Onyx walked with Jinx across the room. "May we continue?"

"Yes." Jinx led her to the bondage bed. He placed her hands on the vinyl cushion. "Up. I'll help you." He guided her onto the soft surface.

"Hands and knees, girl," Zeph said. "You want to orgasm?"

Jinx practically answered for her. Why? He needed to come, too. He helped her settle on the bondage bed. "Good?"

The bit of tenderness belonged in the scene, but wasn't unusual. A good Dom cared for his or her sub, and ensured their safety. She might not belong to them yet, but she had potential and he wanted her.

"I'm good," she replied, slipping out of the scene for a moment. "Thank you, Sir."

He patted her ass, then yielded to Zeph. He and his business partner-slash-best friend had known each other since elementary school. They'd been friends for years and always did things together. Where one went, the other wasn't far behind. For a while, rumors had swirled about their involvement going deeper than friendship.

They hadn't been lovers. They simply worked together and had formed a deeply special bond. They were brothers of the heart. When they found the right person, they'd be the triad they all deserved.

Zephyr stood beside the bed and twirled the crop. "You're a beautiful woman. Love the way your ass reddens when you're spanked. Time to count, girl. Count." He brought the crop down five times on her ass, then smoothed the pad across her abused skin.

Jinx said nothing as he turned on the vibrator and slid it over her pussy a second time. He pinched and rolled her nipple in his free hand. Touching her pleased him.

She trembled. "One, two, three, four, five, Sir. Thank you, Sirs. May I have another?" She groaned and bowed her head. "My God."

"Yeah?" Jinx gritted his teeth. The bone-deep desire to bury himself in her nearly overwhelmed him. He continued to vibrate her. "Tell me — tell us — what you want."

"Tell us," Zeph said. "Girl?"

"I need to come, Sirs. May I come, please? Sirs?" She shivered and backed into the crop. "I forgot how many spanks. Punish me, Sirs. I need..." She bowed her head. When she flexed her hands, her trembling increased.

"Come for us," Zeph said. He smoothed his palm over her ass. "Let go."

"Yes, girl. Let go." Jinx placed the vibrator along her pussy lips. "Yes."

She groaned louder. "Thank you, Sirs." She arched her back, then leaned forward and rested her head on the cushion. Her cream slid down her inner thigh. "Thank you."

"Good girl." Jinx turned off the vibrator. He tossed the toy aside and scooped her into his arms. The cuffs clinked and rattled with each step as he carried her to the couch.

Once he sat down with her in his arms, he arranged her feet onto Zephyr's legs when his best friend joined them.

Zephyr removed her shoes and massaged her feet. "Good girl."

She rested her head on Jinx's shoulder. She said nothing as she curled into him.

"Close your eyes. It's going to be bright." Jinx removed the blindfold, then tossed it aside. "Take your time."

"Thank you," she murmured.

"You've pleased us," Jinx said. "Made us quite happy." He petted her hair as he held her. He'd hold her for as long as she wanted. Forever, if she asked.

"Give yourself time to come down, Zephyr said. He continued to rub her feet. "Rest until you feel ready. We enjoyed playing with you and want to do it again. We want to see you many times. You're one in a million."

"What if I never feel ready?" she murmured. "What if I want to stay right here?"

"Then stay." He met Zeph's gaze. He didn't want her to go, either. Part of him wanted to claim her now, but another part of him wanted to wait. She had him all churned up.

"Would you want a Sir? If given the chance?" Zeph asked. "Do you want to be collared? Talk to us, girl."

She lifted her head. "What?"

"Do you want to be collared? Eventually?" Jinx asked, pushing his anxiety aside. If Zephyr was game, then he could be, too. He rather liked her.

"I do, but not so soon." She sat up. "I should get back to work."

It was almost like a switch had flipped in her and the façade, which had dropped for a while, was back.

"Work? I thought you were a club slave, but that's not a job, per se." Jinx didn't understand, but he wasn't a fan of how she'd switched back to the role of the perfect sub. Something wasn't right.

"Yes." She left his lap and scooped up her shoes from the floor. "I need to distribute drinks until two."

"It's not a bar." Zephyr jumped to his feet. "Are you employed here? Beyond being a club slave?"

"Sort of." She put the shoes on, then bowed. "I can't explain it and refuse to let you know. It's my problem, not yours. I'm sorry I won't go into details, but thank you, Sirs. I should go."

"Wait." Jinx left his seat. "Stop." *God damn it.* He needed her to come back. Like right now.

"I can't." She hesitated, then scrambled out of the room. The door clicked as it closed.

The silence enveloped him. He turned his attention to Zephyr. "What just happened?"

"I don't know."

He scratched his forehead. "Well, shit." He had his misgivings about claiming her so fast, but that didn't mean he wanted her to walk away so quickly, either.

"Yeah." Zephyr shook his head. "This makes no sense, but tells me we need to investigate this more. Something's off."

"It is." He wished he knew.

Zephyr's phone buzzed and he groaned. "I should've known." He checked the screen. "Looks like we've got to go back to the real world. The accountant wants to discuss some discrepancies in the books in the morning. I thought we'd sorted this shit out when we hired the accountants."

"Can't blame them if the crews are fudging something. To be honest, we should be grateful they've caught the issues." He shifted his pants to alleviate the crush against his groin. "Let's go." This wasn't how he wanted to end the evening, but he had no choice.

Jinx left the club with Zephyr and his thoughts kept returning to Onyx. They'd been together not half an hour before and he wanted to replay every second. Part of him was ready to head home. He needed a decent night's sleep and could use a drink. The rest of him — the biggest part of him — wanted to go right back into the building and demand that Onyx come with them. She didn't belong at the club. She might like the play, but she couldn't hide that sadness.

The club wasn't a home. Not an actual one. But their home wasn't a proper one without their third.

He wasn't entirely convinced she was the one destined to be their third, but she was pretty damn close.

He settled on the passenger seat in the truck. He and Zephyr could afford to have a driver and be chauffeured everywhere, but they both preferred to drive themselves. He liked the truck better than the sports cars because the truck wasn't flashy. They'd bought the vehicle back in the early days of their business and he hadn't wanted to sell it. Why sell a piece of their history?

"You're quiet." Zephyr climbed behind the wheel. "You didn't enjoy yourself?"

The erection he needed to relieve sure signaled his enjoyment. But he had to think the situation through. "Tonight?"

"Yeah." Zephyr didn't put the key in the ignition. He turned in his seat and faced Jinx. "You didn't? I loved it. I want to turn her over my knee and spank her ass red all over again, then bring her home. I want her as the ultimate trophy, naked and always at our discretion."

He liked the sound of that. "I enjoyed myself." To be honest, he was rather overwhelmed.

"Okay? Just enjoyed?" Zephyr shook his head. "I know you better than you know yourself. Better than I know myself. You had the time of your life, but you're being quiet. This isn't like you. Normally, you're talking my head off and I'm the one who doesn't speak.

You'd better spill. She's more than we expected and that's something to discuss."

"What's to tell?" He needed to stop hesitating and figure himself out. "I liked it a lot. She blew my mind and I liked how we became three so easily."

"I see." Zephyr narrowed his eyes. "But you're concerned?"

"I am." That was one way to put it.

"Why?"

"Why?" He sighed. "I'm concerned because I like her and I'm afraid of how much I'm already attracted to her. I've never felt like this before. Other women were fine, but she's managed to get her hooks in me. It's been one scene. We haven't even kissed her and yet, I can't think about anything else."

"You, too?"

"Yeah." He shook his head. "But I'm also afraid. I'm worried she might not want to belong to us. Might not want to be our sub. What if she's only interested in our money? What if she's only after us because she wants a payday? She might not want to be our third."

"Whoa," Zephyr said. "We haven't brought up money, or offered for her to be the third."

"I know, but what if she gave herself over to us because she knew who we were and she wanted status?" He knew better. He'd watched her speak to Zephyr and heard her hesitation. Anyone who really knew their identity and wanted them for money alone wouldn't have deferred so much. She'd have been bolder, pushier. She'd have demanded something from them.

Or this was an elaborate charade to make them think she was so compliant. Once she got them to buy her story, she'd change. Others had, so why not her?

"Jinx?" Zephyr rattled his keys. "Hey. You're worried about something that hasn't happened yet. Something that may never happen. It's a lot of mights and a lot of worry. You're overthinking this."

"I am." He knew that.

"You're freaking out and it's not like you," Zephyr said. "You're the one who moves on instinct and takes charge. You take what you want. You don't wait."

"And you do. You're the timid one." Their opposite personalities worked in business and their friendship. They'd figured out when Jinx's boldness needed to be upfront, and when to let Zephyr's more reserved approach work.

"Then listen to me. I want to research her a bit. She's hiding something, but I don't get the feeling it's a love of money. Yes, we should take time to get to know her, but she's special and she makes us happy. She makes us better. Once we get a bead on her, we make another move and get her the fuck out of this club. It's not a bad place, but it's not somewhere for her to be. She's fragile, yet tough as nails and deserves more."

"Agreed."

"So let's research her. That's one thing we both do well, and we'll figure out who she really is. Once we do, then we move forward." Zephyr stuffed the keys into the ignition and started the truck. "Ready?"

"I am." Truth be told, he appreciated the straight talk from Zephyr. He had the peace of mind he needed and a plan for the near future. Things would work out because he knew they would, but also because he and Zephyr would make them work.

Chapter Three

She had to be flying. Still. The scene had been two days ago, and yet she couldn't get it out of her mind. Jinx and Zephyr were more than she'd ever imagined. They hadn't kissed her or even promised more than another chance, but that didn't matter.

"You're in a good mood," Sadie said. "I've seen that smile."

"I'm happy." She changed the filter in the drink machine nozzle. "Should I not be?"

"No." Sadie stared at her. "I heard a rumor."

"Around here? No." She rolled her eyes. She and Sadie worked in a club and everyone talked about each other. It was nothing new for a rumor to start over the most mundane situation.

"Aren't you going to ask me what I heard?"

"No." She shied away from gossip. The less she knew, the better.

"Not even if it's about you?"

"Nope." A rumor about her? Figured. She'd been taken to a private room by two of the most eligible bachelors at the club. Everyone had noticed, no one knew what had happened and they all had their ideas.

"Fine," Sadie said. "I'll tell you anyway."

"I don't want to know." Truly. She had no need to get her hopes up or dashed because of speculation.

"Too late. I'm telling, because you've managed to snag Mr. Collins and Mr. Anderson, the most sought-after men in the club. It's going around that they collared you, but it's been kept on the down low."

"Please." She groaned to hide her slight enjoyment. It'd be nice if the men were truthful in their desire to collar her, but she refused to get her hopes up. They might not even come back to the club.

"That's all? Please? You're so sarcastic. Come on." Sadie sank onto the stool as Onyx emptied the dishwasher. "Can't you show some excitement?"

"Since little of that happened? No, I can't."

"They snagged you."

"They did. Everyone saw us leave together, so yes, that's true." She placed the hot glasses on the towel to cool before stacking them.

"Okay."

She sighed. "There was no drama, so this is me putting it to rest. They did choose me to go to the room with them. I'll confirm that."

"Good. The claiming?"

"Never happened." She stacked the rest of the glasses in the rack, then placed everything in the bus tub into the dishwasher. "Not a bit."

"You're full of it. I have it on good authority it did happen."

"You do?" She added the soap, then rinse agent before closing the door. "Better than a participant?"

"Yes."

She'd love to know who it was, mostly because Sadie was full of bullshit. "Okay?"

"So you want the rest?"

"No." Not a bit.

"Too bad. I know and I won't tell you. So there." Sadie shrugged and walked away.

Fine by me. So far, Sadie's intel had taught her nothing. Onyx stocked the bar with salt, limes and lemons, then ensured the syrup was full in the various canisters of the drink machine. When finished behind the bar, she grabbed the sweeper from the closet. The dedicated cleaning crew would be in later, but she preferred to keep the place better than she'd found it.

Sadie returned to the bar and grumbled. "They didn't claim you?"

"No."

"Didn't beg you to be theirs?"

She tapped the button to release the sweeper handle, but didn't turn on the machine. "No."

"Didn't tell you that they'd be back?"

"No." The longer she stood there, the more she realized what was going on. This was a fishing expedition. Why ask a hundred questions without having the actual truth? If Sadie pecked at Onyx enough, then she'd have to crack, right?

Wrong. Onyx wouldn't crack.

"Why won't you tell me what happened?" Sadie whined. "I got some story, a bunch of rumors and half-truths. Spill so I know what happened."

"There's nothing to spill." Plus, she loved the satisfaction of annoying Sadie.

"Okay," Sadie said. "Here's what I know. You dispute it if it's wrong."

She'd never let up.

"No answer is a good one. Okay, so they chose you and took you to the other room, yes?" Sadie asked.

"They invited me, yes." She flexed her hand on the handle of the sweeper.

"Then they decided they wanted you and put in a word with the heads of the club. They're coming back tonight to take what's theirs, because you left an impression," Sadie said. "How'd you do it? The most valuable unattached men in the club and they chose you. Tell me your secrets."

"What's to tell?"

"Everything. It's just…it's…I don't like it."

She drummed her fingertips on the handle. "Let me guess. It's not fair? You're pretty and I'm just…boring? You should've gotten the high dollar men?"

"I never said that."

"Then why?"

"I deserve a sugar daddy or two."

Sadie deserved to be humbled a bit. "You know they might have chosen me because I was available? It's possible I just happened to be the girl on the floor. You were busy and I wasn't. I was here. It could've been anyone, but I was here," she said. "Okay? Does that satisfy you?"

Sadie crinkled her nose. "No."

"Why not?" It'd been the truth.

"I was here and they didn't chose me."

"You were in a scene."

"So?"

She shifted her weight from her left foot to her right. "Maybe they wanted someone a little more humble?" Sadie was anything but. "I don't know, and I didn't ask."

"Wait." Sadie stood in front of the sweeper. "You really think they looked me over and passed me by because I'm not humble?"

"It's possible." *Quite.*

"They don't know me. I'm the Queen of Humble. I'm the most humble sub here." Sadie inched away. "I'm so humble, it's scary."

Oh, it was. Onyx shook her head and tapped the handle of the sweeper. She had things to do. "Maybe next time."

"I did hear they're coming back."

"They could be." Of course they'd come back. They were frequent attendees. She didn't want to care that they were and didn't want to care that they might not choose her. She'd prefer not to be a one-off, but she doubted they'd decide to have more with her. "Why don't you prep for it? I hear room nine is good for attracting people." She'd never been invited to room nine, only passed through. But then there were lots of rooms she'd never enjoyed.

"I will." Sadie paused. "But if they *did* choose you and you *did* decide to be with them, you're lucky and going to be spoiled. They're gazillionaires."

"They're just guys." She knew the basics of their net worth and it meant nothing to her. She wasn't attracted to money. Sure, she'd like to be a kept woman, but it wasn't a big deal. Sadie needed the adulation. Onyx wanted love and passion, but she didn't demand it. If she was going to have it, though, she welcomed them with open arms.

"Just guys?" Sadie clicked her tongue. "You'd minimize anything."

"No." She considered herself pragmatic. There was no point in expecting what wouldn't happen.

"When they come in tonight and collar you, you owe me." Sadie pointed to her. "You do."

"Why? What'd you do to get them to pay attention to me? You did nothing." No encouragement. Hell, if given the chance, Sadie would've pushed her aside in a hot minute to get to them.

Sadie crinkled her lips, then blushed. "Maybe I didn't, but you still owe me."

"For what?"

"For not being out front and being noticed first." Sadie turned on her heel. "I need to go."

"Have fun." She switched from the broom to the vacuum, flicked the switch on the machine before pushing the vacuum around the carpet. As she cleaned, her thoughts turned to the evening with Jinx and Zephyr. They knew how to touch her, please her and make her beg. Knew how to respect her, too.

Finding men who could be respectful and forceful wasn't easy—not for her. They wanted things. Expected them.

She'd loved her modeling days, but some aspects still bothered her. She winced at the memory of the comments made about her body and intelligence. About what she did and didn't do.

Wearing pretty clothes, posing for photos, assisting the designers...it was all fun and exciting. The other things she'd been forced to do weren't so much. She'd been championed for her leggy frame and simple looks. The designers liked tall, thin bodies and blonde hair. Her looks were her biggest asset, but they'd also been her curse.

She never wanted to revisit that curse, but she lived it every day.

She finished sweeping, then put the vacuum back in the closet. One day, she'd have her debt to the club paid off and she'd be free.

One day.

"Onyx." Keifer Jones, the club owner, strolled into the room. "I see you're hard at work. Nice and clean."

"I try, Sir." She winced. He'd paid to keep her out of trouble and out of the darker clubs after the scandals hit. He'd paid to keep Nacin at bay, too. The scandals had nearly killed her career and Keifer had offered a lifeline—if he wanted something from her, then she had to comply.

"You do well." Keifer rounded the bar. "I heard you've attracted attention."

"I guess I did." She'd never had long conversations with him. He liked to throw his money around and argue his worth, but he didn't like to talk, so him keeping the conversation going confused her. "Was it wrong?"

"Not entirely." Keifer leaned on the bar and a predatory look filled his eyes. "You could bring in decent money."

"I could?" She didn't like the sound of that. There wasn't a plan at all, but his words scared her.

"If the players who chose you the other night show interest again, I'll expect some payment."

"Because they've got money." She nodded. "You think they'll give it to me? I don't want to beg them. It's not me. Besides, they wanted a toy."

"They'll pay dearly for you."

"Nah." She pulled the curtain across the front of the closet, obscuring it from view. "It was one time and I doubt they'll give me money." Once they found out how much she owed, they'd be turned off. They might be put off by the fact she owed Keifer anything at all. If they bothered to come back, they'd want someone better—like Sadie. Someone with less baggage.

"You discount yourself."

"You've discounted me, too." At this rate, she'd be paying for her protection until she was a little old lady in handcuffs.

"I keep you grounded." Keifer reached for her. "Why don't you let me reduce some of your debt?"

She stayed out of reach. "What do you mean?" She wasn't interested, but had to hear him out. She could end up in deeper trouble if she resisted. "How?"

"You could offer to serve me." His eyes flashed. "Or you could entice them to spend more money here. Spend a lot more. Like maybe even pay to renovate a room, or create a new one. They'll spend a lot if you put on the charm."

She tried to keep her disgust at bay. She could reduce her debt if she played up to the Doms and brought in cash. Or she could submit to Keifer.

Neither sounded good.

Her stomach churned. She'd done enough while modeling to get attention. She'd played up to plenty of men who were gross, just to get a dinner, a night out, or a few bucks. She never slept with them, but she allowed them to have her on their arm for the evening. They knew she needed money and they'd exploited her, which was the reason she'd gotten hooked up with Keifer. She'd needed bailed out.

She wasn't interested in Keifer, or in submitting to him, because he slept with almost every one of the subs in the building and took advantage of them. Now that Darius had given Keifer the job of overseeing the place, Keifer took advantage. Darius kept the girls safe. Keifer was another story.

"See what you can do." Keifer caressed her hand. "I know you'll come through for the club. You always do."

"I do." This was no time to argue. "Thank you, Sir." He wasn't her Sir, but he demanded she address him as such.

"By the way, the guys will be here and have requested you." Keifer offered his completely fake thousand-watt smile. "You know what to do."

"I do." They'd asked for her? Holy cow. The concept was rather exciting, but she wondered if he'd told them to choose her? Probably had. "I'm finished for now, Sir."

"Good. I expect to see you do your job." Keifer kissed her on the cheek. "Good girl."

"Thank you." She wanted to throw up. She wasn't happy about being used this way. God, he disgusted her. She left the main bar and headed to her locker before leaving the club. The second she stepped out into the chilly early evening, she wished she'd bought a thicker coat. She clutched the garment closed as she rushed across the parking garage floor. When she reached her car, she glanced around. She'd been taught to pay attention to her surroundings. For all she knew, Nacin's goons had tailed her. They'd assaulted her before when she hadn't complied.

Keifer had had to intervene.

She checked her car, then her tires before unlocking the door. A shiver ran the length of her spine. She didn't want to drag Jinx and Zephyr into her problems. Between the other men of wealth chasing her, Nacin demanding sexual favors she refused to give, and Keifer pushing her…she wasn't sure she could keep her mind intact.

The whole situation was a disaster and she had no idea how to end it. She'd been given suggestions, but none were palatable.

She opened her car door, then hesitated when she heard the screech of tires. No one was supposed to be on the parking garage floor without a special membership card, but that didn't mean she was safe. She swore she heard a click.

Fuck. Her mind raced with every possibility of what could be happening.

"Onyx?"

"Yes?" She trembled. "If you're going to kill me, just do it. Don't make me beg or cry." Tears slipped down her cheeks and she refused to turn around. If they weren't going to kill her, they'd see her back and she'd prove they were cowards to shoot someone in a defenseless position.

"What?" The man speaking to her, the one with the sexy gravelly voice strode around her. Zephyr. She blinked as he crinkled his brow. "Who wants to kill you? Tell me."

She'd stepped in it now. "It's nothing." She shook her head. No need to tell him about her troubles. Not right now. "Forget it." She'd made a big mistake in bringing up the past, even in passing. No, she'd keep her problems to herself. It was the best way. *The only way.*

"Forget it? You're asking us to forget your sweet smile. I can't understand why that smile is gone or why you're scared, but I want to know." Zephyr offered his hand. "Give us a chance. I'd like to know why you're so freaked. If we can help, we will."

She should let them help. *Should.* "Have you talked to Keifer?" If they had, they'd know the situation and wouldn't be so kind to her. They'd see right through the charade.

"We've talked to him." Jinx stood next to her car. "I don't care what Keifer says. I care about you and that look in your eyes that tells me you'll run. I don't like that look, so I'll ask you the same question. Who wants to kill you?"

"It's nothing." Not a damn thing she wanted to explain. She never wanted to explain it. How could she? How was she going to tell them about the things she'd done? The things she'd worked so hard to forget? It was impossible.

"I don't like games and I'm not sure why I can't shake the feeling there's more going on here. Why doesn't one of us ride with you and we'll get out of here?" Zephyr asked. "The truck's right over there. Want to ride with Jinx in the truck while I drive your car?"

"You'd trust your life in my car?" she blurted. She snapped her mouth shut. Good fucking God. Of all the things she could've said.

"I shouldn't?" Zephyr shook his head. "I've had enough of this."

"I know, and I'm sorry." She hated getting emotional, but she'd had more than she could handle. She expected to be told to get lost because she was more trouble than she was worth. Once she started crying, she couldn't stop. "I didn't agree to entice you. I don't want to be that person. I'm sorry. I'm not."

Jinx and Zephyr shared a glance.

"I didn't agree to it, but he put me up to it. I'm not that girl." The tears fell harder. "I didn't accept those favors and didn't expect them. God, I'm not that girl." She wasn't talking about anything they'd given her, but the past had never gone away.

"Okay." Jinx enfolded her in his arms. He petted her hair as she sobbed against his chest. "Slow down."

She wanted to go. No, she needed… If only she could turn the tears off quickly and move forward. She continued to sob, opening the floodgates on frustration and anger that she'd held in place for so many years.

"I don't understand what happened, but we'll get to the bottom of it. Not here." Jinx guided her to the other vehicle. "You'll sit between us and we'll be fine."

"Are you sure?" she mumbled. "I'm trouble."

"You might be, but you're worth the trouble." Zephyr opened the door for her. "We truly don't mind."

"No?" It wasn't possible.

"We're tougher than you think," Jinx said.

"And we don't put up with shit, especially when someone important to us is in trouble," Zephyr said. "Get in. We're going somewhere less noisy, nosy and open."

She hadn't paid attention to the noise in the garage, but knew there were cameras around. Keifer had probably already seen everything. She climbed into the truck. It wasn't a fancy vehicle, not loaded or overblown, like she'd expected.

Then again, Jinx and Zephyr weren't anything like she'd expected.

Good, really. She liked the change of pace. She settled between them and her heart raced. She didn't belong here—not with two wealthy men, not being rescued. Not being appreciated.

She'd learned to be quietly pretty. Another sweet smile in the crowd of tall, slender models.

So much for being ordinary.

Zephyr sat behind the wheel and Jinx sat on her other side. Zephyr engaged the engine. "Do you have anything in your car you need to grab? Is it locked? I'll assume you've got a fob?"

She'd forgotten all about the car. She tapped the button and prayed the vehicle didn't explode. When it beeped and the lights flashed, she relaxed a tiny bit. She'd probably get charged for leaving the car there overnight, but what was new? Keifer charged her for everything, if he didn't take the payments out of her wages. Another addition to her already high debts. There wasn't much she could do about it now.

She clicked her belt into place and forced her thoughts from Keifer. "Why are you here tonight? The club is open and you should be inside playing. Aren't you going to scene?"

"We came here tonight to see you," Zephyr said and drove out of the parking garage. "I guess he didn't tell you?"

"He? Who? Keifer? No." She'd have dressed for a scene if she'd known they were coming that night to play.

"Rat bastard. I knew he'd keep it a secret," Jinx said. "He's probably thinking he's got a racket in place. The man's one gigantic con."

Con? She agreed a thousand percent. If there was a way to make money, Keifer would find it. He'd exploit it. He'd be...a rat bastard.

"We arrived tonight to talk to you about making the scene last a little longer and what you might have for expectations. We'd like to play again, and soon," Jinx said. "What do you think?"

"You would? With me?" She should stop blurting things out.

"Uh-huh." Zephyr sped down the main street away from the club. "There's more to life than being a house slave. You should have better. What do you say?"

With them? She said yes. "I'll hear you out." She'd been trained to be way too skittish and concerned with decisions, but she'd been burned too many times not to be.

"Good." Zephyr turned onto a side street. "We'll get to the bottom of this killing issue and set some rules before we move forward. Trust me, I'm glad we got away from that club. If Darius was still here managing, we'd stay. Keifer is up to no good."

"He is." She shifted her gaze between Jinx and Zephyr. She had time with them, wasn't at the club and could breathe for a moment. She didn't have the closure she needed from her past, but she saw a glimmer of light. There just might be an end to her problems.

Might.

But she had time with Jinx and Zephyr.

Hot damn.

Chapter Four

Zephyr bit back his anger as he drove out of town toward the mansion. He'd done his due diligence when he'd researched her. She'd been a model, and damn good at it. She'd done many runway shows and worked for large companies. But she'd been the target of some very wealthy men. Not just targeted, but annoyed, bothered, assaulted and most likely abused. Seeing the information, even if some of it was simply rumor, pissed him off. Jinx hadn't been any less angry. No one deserved to be treated that way—wealth and power or not.

What pissed Zephyr off the most was Keifer. The ass had come in, demanded attention and promised he could fix this for her. No doubt he'd dazzled her with promises of cash and a way out. He'd probably told her he'd pay her debts and save her from the troubles she'd incurred, like Nacin.

Zephyr had thought about Nacin, too. Nacin was just another rich man who believed every pretty girl owed him. He should be able to touch them as he pleased and they should bow down to him. Should feel indebted to him and should want him to fawn over her. They should be flattered by his lizard-like behavior. The entitlement annoyed Zephyr.

Most people annoyed him, but he had even less time for users.

He stole a glance at Onyx. God, she was a sight. When she went into a room, he'd bet the place lit up. He liked her smile and wanted to see it again at full wattage.

He hated that he'd had to research her, but he insisted on knowing what he was in for. She looked great and played well in the club, but if he faced problems, he'd rethink the connection.

The more he researched her, the more he realized her issues weren't of her own making, except with Keifer. He couldn't blame her for her actions there. She'd thought he'd given her a lifeline.

Instead, he'd chained her in a prison he'd created for her.

Zephyr shook his head. He knew so much and nothing at all about her. Her photos captivated him. There were plenty of pretty girls, but she had a particular sparkle. He didn't need a model for their business, but she'd be a good image person. Hell, he might employ her for that reason—to make her the face of the business. She'd be good for television advertising and in print media.

The plan could work.

First, he needed to get beyond her defenses.

Jinx might have better ideas than him, anyway. Jinx was more likely to jump in with both feet, where

Zephyr planned. Jinx moved with gut instinct and most of the time his guts were right.

But even he sensed Jinx's hesitation. They had to figure out what was going on with Onyx before they could fix it—if she even wanted them to do so.

At least there was time to sort everything out.

He pulled into the drive, then headed up to the house before parking in the garage. As the door went down, bathing them in semi-darkness, she tensed.

"We're home," he said and turned off the engine. Neither she nor Jinx had spoken throughout the trip. Were they stuck in thought? Could be. "Are we good?"

"Yeah," Jinx said with a chuckle. "I got stuck in my own head. Should've been more chatty."

He'd assumed as much. "Onyx?"

"What?" She stared at him, wide-eyed. "Why don't you just take me back? I don't belong here."

"No?" He didn't buy it. "Well, you're here and I'm not going back to the club again tonight. I've had enough of that place."

"Agreed." Jinx opened the truck door and checked his phone. "Come on. We'll show you around." He slid out of the truck, then growled. "Strike that. Zeph will give you the grand tour. I'll be in the office. There's apparently an issue with the copy on some print advertising. I swear, they don't check them before they send shit out."

Zephyr understood all too well. They had good people in place to keep the business thriving. Sure, they owned it, but the various players knew their roles— except every so often, something dropped. When that happened, he and Jinx got irked. "Take your time."

"I hope not much." Jinx rushed into the house, leaving them alone.

"So..." She clutched her bag. "Haven't changed your mind, have you?"

"Nope. Should I?" He expected answers from her, but he had to be patient.

"Yes."

"Why?" He stayed in the truck with her. "No one will hurt you here. No one will give you any grief. Just talk. I'm good at listening and can promise I won't try anything. I know you've heard it all before, but we're legit." He should be dealing with a fire of his own, but the other problems would wait. His life didn't revolve around the landscaping business.

"Sir."

"We're not in a scene. I'm Zephyr, or Zeph. Please." He held out his hand. She didn't place hers in his right away, but did relent. "Good. Now, talk to me." He laced his fingers with hers because he liked holding her hand. She smelled good, felt even better and he liked the fire in her eyes.

"I can't." She shook her head. "I need to get out of here before you change your mind."

"About what?" There was patience, but there were times when people could be a tad needy. He had to figure out the balance. "I researched you." It was risky to admit, but she deserved to know the truth from the start.

"You what?"

"Jinx moves on impulse and instinct. I don't. I like to know what I'm getting into before I move, so I did my research on you." He might have stepped in it up to his eyeballs, but he also wanted to protect her. He'd considered his options and this felt like the right path to take.

Her eyes widened. "And you didn't like what you saw?"

"I never said that." *Not even close.*

"Stop."

"I won't lie. I didn't like what I saw because I saw things happening at the hands of someone else. Those men were jerks and you should've been given respect, so yeah, that's what I didn't like. The rest? I saw someone doing the best she could and trying, despite the odds. That's impressive because a lot of people fold when faced with that kind of pressure."

She rolled her eyes. "I'm not impressive."

"You may not think so, but you are. We chose you at the club because you captivated us. That's why we made the move and I'm glad we did. It was the best decision we could, even if you don't agree with us. Now, talk to me. Let Jinx and me in because we're here to help."

She sighed. "So what do you want me to do?"

"I'd like you to come with me as I show you around the house." He caressed her hand. "Come on."

She allowed him to lightly tug her out of the truck and to her feet. He continued to hold her hand as he led her into the house. He might not be the richest man, but he and Jinx had a great home and he wanted to share it with her.

"This is insane." She kicked out of her shoes, then padded with him through the kitchen. "Wow."

"What?"

"This house. It's huge." She leaned into him. "I don't know if I belong in such a nice place."

"You do." He grinned to himself. "I've seen your photos. You did good work. Those pictures are... I'm jealous because you make posing look easy. I'm terrible when someone tries to take my picture."

"Why?"

"I tend to unwittingly make a strange face, blink at the wrong time, close my eyes or look away." He shrugged and steered her into the drawing room.

"What's this?" She pulled away and wandered around the space. "It's fantastic. So much natural light and the landscapes... Do you use this room for photography?"

"Jinx likes to draw in here. When he's stressed or frustrated, he comes in here to create art. Every so often, he paints. He hasn't in quite a while, though." He knew damn well why. Jinx hadn't been inspired lately. "He's done some prints for comic books, too. The art, and something I can't remember what it's called for the books."

"Inking? Or does he do panel art?" She faced him. "I did a few photo shoots in superhero garb for a perfume campaign."

"Yeah?" He'd seen the shots and she'd floored him. She made the tight clothing and ridiculous colors look fantastic.

"Uh-huh." She grinned and a little of her fire came back—at least as much as he could see. "I liked that shoot because we used fire, flash pots and special lighting."

"Did you?" The information wasn't news to him, but he wanted her to be comfortable and he liked how she spoke about herself.

"I did." She inched up to him. "Does it sound bad if I say I miss the game?"

"Which one?" He had an idea what she meant.

"The modeling game. The fuss, the jobs, the hustling to shoots and need for perfection. All the dressing up was so much fun."

He sank onto the arm of the overstuffed chair. "You were good."

"Yeah?" She snorted. "Not good enough to stay in the spotlight. Everyone wants to be the next pretty girl. The hottest one and there's always someone waiting to be next. It's cutthroat."

"I'm sure it is. The landscaping industry is, too." He loved listening to her. "We had to claw to get where we are."

She sat on the cushions and faced him, tucking one leg under the other. "One time, I got to do a lingerie shoot. It was a big conglomerate company and they catered the shoot. I mean, really did it up big. They demanded a lot, like specific poses in specific garments. It was sexy and fun and I felt like a princess in those feathers, beads…rhinestones."

He'd bet it was fun to dress up. He'd love to make her feel that desire and delight, too. "You like being pretty?"

"I do." She blushed. "Not just as a sub, but I love that, too. The fancy dresses and the couture stuff is fantastic. I haven't been to a banquet or evening out in a long time."

"No?" She should be dressed in jewels and sequins. Right now, he wanted a few more answers. "Would you tell me why you're afraid of being killed? You belong in photos and modeling, while living your life. Not afraid."

She tensed. "I can't."

"You can." He'd been delicate, but he had to be firmer with her. "You're safe here. Doesn't matter what you did. We care about what's going on right now, and you're with us now. Let us in so we can help you. We'll protect you."

"I've heard that before."

"I know."

"Sir."

"Zephyr or Zeph. I insist."

She sighed. "Fine, Zephyr."

"Will you tell me? I don't know how to make you understand we're not here to hurt or exploit you."

She stared at him and seemed to curl into herself.

"I know Keifer has something on you. I know he's pulling a bullshit stunt, too. What I can't figure out is why he's doing this. What's he going to gain?" There. He'd been blunt with her. It had to work eventually.

"You know?"

"I do." He'd said he'd done his research. "He doesn't know what Jinx and I do, which is important. If he's in the dark, then all the better. He thrives on knowing everything and I won't let him."

"You won't?" She scrubbed both hands over her face. "I hope you're right."

"I am." He never said something without being right and having the facts. Call it his control-freak nature, but he needed to know everything. He knew a con when he saw one and Keifer was the ultimate con man. He'd conned his way into managing the club because he'd claimed he knew how to better than Darius and could give Darius a break from the stress. *Right...*

"Okay." She sighed again. "I'm tired of hiding it and running away."

He offered his hand again. This time, she reached for him and grasped his fingers.

"I started modeling at fourteen. My mother encouraged me because I was so much taller than everyone else, and all legs. I knew how to move because I'd been a dancer and I guess I looked older than fourteen because I got a lot of jobs for older girls. I ended up working frequently until I turned eighteen. I didn't realize at the time that I worked so hard so I could afford my mother a better life. Turned out she'd pocketed most of my money, which sucked. I had to build myself back up all on my own, so I headed to New York and pounded the pavement."

"We've done that—pounded the pavement. We started with two mowers and a boatload of desire." He remembered their early days fondly. Starting had been a struggle, but so worth it.

"Yeah?" Her smile returned for a split-second. "I went to the big city after I graduated and put myself out there. I did any job I could get. I worked solid, but it wasn't always the safest work. But I built myself up and did some big shoots. I had my own apartment and a decent car, too," she said. "Then it happened."

"What?" She had him captivated.

"I got to do some darker shots. I said I'd take anything as long as it meant work, so when the fetish stuff rolled in, I still did it. Most of the work was artsy, not lascivious. I didn't play much back then because I didn't want marks on my body, but being pretty and wearing those sexy clothes or whatever wasn't bad. Wasn't perfect, either. I had men approach me because they thought I modeled fetish stuff and must want them to touch me. I must want them to make comments. They should be entitled to grab me and pinch, but I should also accept it because they're rich men. They think they're better than everyone else."

"They're not." He knew that. "Anyone who believes they're entitled like that isn't a man."

"I wish you'd have been there." She shrugged and shook her head. "Maybe you'd have joined in."

"Never." He could be a son of a bitch when he wanted to, but he never took advantage of people. "I'm not that guy. I'd be the one to step in, though. I'd push them away."

"It would've been nice if you'd have been there. Maybe he'd have backed off," she said.

"What did they do?" he whispered. "Talk to me." If she unburdened, maybe that'd help.

"Touched me without my okay. Kissed me without permission. One tried to rape me." She shivered. "That's why Keifer's involved."

"Keifer tried to...?" He couldn't say the words, much less fathom the moment.

"No. Nacin. George Nacin." Her shivering increased.

He gathered her in his arms. "I'm here. Jinx is here. We've got you and we're not letting you down." He petted her hair. He'd do his best to protect her. Nacin could be dangerous, but also foolish. He could be ruthless, too. Nacin demanded and rarely had to accept the consequences of his actions.

She dug her nails into his forearm. "He forced his way into my dressing room during a vodka commercial shoot. He busted in and demanded I let him touch me. Acted like I should be happy he wanted to pay me attention."

His heart broke for her and her innocence being stolen in that moment. Sure, she'd had experiences, but no one had the right to push that hard. "You didn't have to tell me, but I'm glad you did. We're here for you." He'd made his own mistakes. "I'm sorry."

"You didn't do that to me." She rested her head on his shoulder. "You weren't him. You're not him."

"No." He kissed the top of her head. "Jesus."

"You're disgusted?"

"No." Far from it. "I admire your strength."

"It wasn't strength." She clutched at his shirt. "I pushed and screamed, but he told me I owed him. I had to do this for him because he was important."

"No, you didn't." He practically growled the words out. He'd known lots of people like Nacin and hated their behavior.

"The last man who told me that...never mind." She shook her head again.

"What'd he say?" He wondered who it was. "Who was it?"

"Keifer."

"You're shitting me." Keifer would say anything to get his way.

"No."

The rotten bastard. He should've known Keifer would be so callous. Keifer wanted to possess her. In a way, so did Zephyr, but he kept quiet. She had to speak at her own pace and he couldn't change her past.

"He said he'd protect me and would keep Nacin from assaulting me again, but he never mentioned the full price it'd cost me," she said. "Nacin left me alone, but I traded one devil for another."

"How?" *The fucker.*

"I work at the club when Keifer wants and am a house slave because he expected it."

"What did you want?"

She sat up and faced him. Her makeup ran in thin black streaks down her cheeks. He dried her tears and she swallowed hard. "I love being at the club to play. It's fun and exciting. There's always something to do and if I'd have been there of my own choice, I don't know that I'd have been a house slave. I'd be a member, though."

"Yeah?" He appreciated her candid nature.

"I like being there, but I wish I hadn't been drawn in—like that. Does that make sense?" She frowned. "I never make much sense."

"You make plenty of sense." Besides, he liked her honesty.

"At least someone gets me."

"Jinx does, too."

"I know." She finally grinned a moment. "But seriously. I like being at the club, but I want my own people. I love to watch, to be shown off, but not passed around. That's what I was expected to do—allow myself to be passed around to any man who walked into the club. I'm not into that kind of kink."

"No one says you should be." He didn't like the idea of sharing her with anyone except Jinx. As he thought about his best friend, it dawned on him that he hadn't seen Jinx in quite a while. They'd have to touch base soon.

"I'll give you this. You're convincing and almost make me think you care." She rubbed her bare arms. "Why are you being so kind to me? You don't owe me anything. Don't have to be nice."

"What if I want to? What if that's what Jinx wants? We see a pretty girl who has captured our heart and we'd like to see her smile. That's what propels us. We'd like to know why you're afraid of being killed and we want to protect you." They'd keep her out of the club and get her into somewhere she belonged — with them.

She narrowed her eyes, then groaned before rubbing her face with both hands. "I've got little to lose."

He hated to hear that. "What do you mean?"

She didn't reply right away and shook her head again. "What the hell...if you can protect me, then I have no choice," she said. "I want to keep breathing and I'd like my life back."

"You deserve it."

"I do." She stared at him. "When I didn't let Nacin stick his hands down my dress or in my crotch, he threatened me. Said he'd kill me if I ever crossed him because no one ever turned him down. No one ever made him look like a fool."

"Because you turned him down?"

"I didn't let the slimy bastard touch me and he threw a tantrum like a child. That's what he really is — a big kid who got his hand slapped and didn't like it. I don't care if he didn't like it. I have the right to stop anyone from touching me in a way I don't appreciate."

"Damn right."

"How dare I not let him do what he thought was his right? How dare I not allow him to abuse me? He was giving me the gift of his attention and favor in that instant. How dare I turn him down when he was bestowing on me the thing I should want the most — his...I don't know."

"He's a bastard. You're smart and deserve better, which is why you turned him down." He clenched his fist. He wanted to ram his hand down Nacin's throat. How would old Nacin like to have something forced on him?

"I said no and that's what fired him up. I fought back, too, but who would believe me? He's had five wives—all bottle blondes—and can't seem to keep a stable relationship. He couldn't stand being told no, which was what made him want to chase me more. No one told him no."

He gritted his teeth. She needed to keep talking, but this pissed him off.

"Keifer claimed he'd protect me, but it involved my submission to him and the club. I'm in debt so far that it's not even funny. That's why I was there tonight. I wasn't playing—I was working and cleaning. I'll be working off my debt until I'm a thousand years old and it's ridiculous."

"It is." She didn't have to pay anyone back for that long.

"I know. I never should've made the deal with the devil, but I thought it was a way out. It was a trap. I went from one bad decision to another. One devil to another, all because I saw no other way out." Tears streamed down her cheeks. "I'm a mess."

"No." He kept her in his arms and held her. She'd done the best she could with shitty options. The situation wasn't going to end well at this rate—not until he and Jinx stepped in. They did want her submission in the bedroom, but that was all. Everywhere else, they wanted her independence and fire. They'd spoil her rotten if she'd let them. First, they had to get her to believe them. She shuddered in his arms as she cried.

"I'm sorry." She clutched at his shirt again. "I don't want to be crying because it's a weakness."

"It's only weakness if you believe it is, and I don't. You're not weak for showing your emotions or breaking for a little while. Sometimes you need to crack in order to heal and move forward, and it's time you allowed yourself to do just that."

"What?"

"Let go of the past, let the hurt go and move forward." It sounded so dumb, though. Like a terribly written greeting card or motivational poster.

"Maybe."

"What if I told you that we want to help you? No strings attached." He could speak confidently because he knew Jinx would agree. She needed to be theirs, but also to be free.

"I'd say you were crazy and not telling me the truth." She stared at him. "You're exhausting me."

"Want to rest? We've got a room made up for you." He'd rather her be between them, but he wasn't that pushy. "You've got privacy, security and can rest."

"I'm a prisoner?"

That question irritated him a bit, but he tamped down his frustration. "You need to be more positive. I get why you're not—after what you've been through, it's expected—but you don't have to be so worried. I promise this is all legit."

She narrowed her eyes for a moment, then picked at the wrinkles in his shirt. "I'm not sure I can believe you, but I'd like to rest. What do I owe you? Submission? Money? To clean your house?"

"Nothing." *No strings.*

"Nothing?"

"Nothing," he repeated. "I want you to be happy and rest. I've got plans for you, and none of it involves you giving up your spark for me."

She opened and closed her mouth, but said nothing.

"It's true. Give us a few days to prove it. Will you?" he asked.

"I can leave whenever I want?"

"Yes." He doubted she would. "I'll arrange for a driver myself to take you back when you want it."

"Okay."

"Okay?"

"Yes." She sighed and sat up straighter. "If I'm going to be in debt to someone, it might as well be you and Jinx."

"I can tell you like us, but you're not financially obligated to us."

"I do like and respect you. And...I don't want a debit."

"We respect you, too, which is why there's nothing to be repaid." He led her to the guest suite and kept the door open. "Why don't you relax? You can leave at any time, are free, but also have the full use of the house. Does that please you?" He could see whatever she did at any time, but he wasn't worried. Besides, the suite was connected to the master suite and if she decided to stick around, he'd have her moved over in seconds.

"No strings?" She gave him the side-eye look.

"No strings. I need to speak to Jinx because I haven't seen him in a while. Make sure things are okay, you know?" he asked. "But you're free to use the suite and find us if you want to keep talking."

"I'm sure things are fine." She stepped out of her shoes. "May I have my bag? I left it in the other room. And...as long as I'm not a prisoner, I'm fine, too. I'll be okay."

"I never doubted you." He'd have to work hard to gain her trust. She'd been burned before. Practically flambéed. She'd be a challenge, but he and Jinx loved the challenge.

She gave him the side-eye look again, then nodded. "May I have a bath?"

"Of course." Why couldn't she?

"I usually shower at the club because it's cheaper to use the facilities there than the water in my building." She blushed. "That sounds shitty, doesn't it?"

"Sounds like you're really struggling." He wished he hadn't said that. "I mean...it sounds like you're resourceful."

"When all of my extra cash goes to paying Keifer for protection, yeah, I'm struggling." She offered a half-smile. "Thank you. It might only be for a few days, but I'll treasure every second."

"You'll love it." Her words irritated him because he knew to his core that she didn't believe him. But he understood. This was a trust situation, and she didn't trust him at all. Soon, she would. He and Jinx would make sure of it. She should be pampered and spoiled. Should know she was loved.

Challenge accepted.

Chapter Five

Jinx threw down the cell phone onto the couch and raked his fingers through his short hair. He'd had enough of playing businessman for one day. They'd hired people to keep the business running, but no one wanted to do their jobs. He hated firing people and getting rid of contractors, but he and Zeph weren't going to pay someone to goof off. If the work wasn't done, then someone would have to get it done. If the job was ignored, then the customer felt the same and they lost jobs.

He scrubbed both hands over his face. He'd have to have a conference with the slate of managers before long.

Zeph strolled into the office. "You disappeared."

"I did, and I'm sorry." Jinx sat on the edge of the desk. "It's a mess. They know how to do the job and don't care."

"Many do, but a few bad apples showed up." Zeph widened his stance and folded his arms. "It can be sorted out."

"I know." This wasn't his arena. Zeph tended to handle the hiring and firing of the contractors. He stuck to design, unless he was required to handle situations. He'd rather be approving design plans or creating custom sketches. "What's the deal with Onyx? I see she's not happy."

"Not happy is an understatement. That woman is burned out and tired. She's scared, too."

"Of us?" *Christ, no.* "What'd we do wrong?"

"We didn't do anything wrong, but she doesn't trust us. She believes we'll use her in the same way Keifer and Nacin did. That ass assaulted her and destroyed her career. Then the bastard had it swept under the rug. I'd bet they worked together. Buried the story so no one believes her."

"What a crock of shit." His irritation turned to anger. "What do we do?"

"Respect her, for one. Get her out of that club for good."

"What's wrong with the club?"

"Nothing, necessarily. The issue is with Keifer and his extortion."

"Oh?" He gripped the edge of his desk. He'd like to hear this, then he'd like to rip Keifer limb from limb.

"He's got her working there, like I assumed. Unpaid actual work. She's a house slave, she cleans and refreshes the bar. She mans the toy chest and more that I don't even know yet. He's got her essentially in servitude for life."

"Why?" If she enjoyed the work or whatever, he'd be fine, but he doubted she did. "Is she his girl?"

"No."

His annoyance grew. "I see. So she's being used."

"He paid off Nacin and I'm looking into it more, but I believe Nacin wanted the assault and when she turned him down, he got angry. Threatened her. Keifer knew what she liked and saw a way to get something for nothing. There's got to be a deeper link there, but I haven't found it yet," Zeph said. "Doesn't matter. It's shitty."

"You smell the stench of extortion a mile away."

"Five hundred miles."

"Yeah." He smelled it, too.

"Then what do we do? Dismember him?"

"Financially, yes."

"I'm game." He'd love to destroy the bully. "What'd he do? Besides the extortion?"

"If it's true that he's got her there under the guise of a job, then it's really extortion. Gotta be. He's got a gorgeous girl to use in advertising and gets to use her good nature. She thinks she's being protected, but I guarantee she's starting to figure this all out. She knows she's being used."

"And she's okay with it?" He doubted that.

"It's not so much that she's okay, but she's afraid to be forceful because that's what's gotten her into this mess in the first place. She pushed Nacin away and got hassled. If she snubs Keifer, she risks being fucked over all over again."

"Then we ruin him. Not the club, but him." He nodded. He could handle a thousand issues with contractors now that he'd been energized by this fight. He and Zeph could be ruthless in business, but they stood up for the little guy. She might not be a guy, but that didn't matter. She deserved better. "I have an idea."

"You do?" Zeph nodded once. "Clue me in."

"Keifer said something about an addition."

Zeph crinkled his brow and said nothing.

"He encouraged me to suggest you and I pay a few dollars to the club. I assumed he wanted us to buy her and I was right. If he cons us, then he's going to use her as the pawn."

Zephyr massaged his temples. "Use her as the bait to reel us in and then get us to dump money into the club?"

"Exactly."

"That's cruel."

"It is if she's not interested, but it sure feels like she's intrigued with us. Not intrigued with malicious intentions, but she's truly interested."

"She is." Zeph snapped his fingers. "Come with me."

He followed his best friend out to the office to the guest quarters. "Is that singing?" he murmured. He swore he heard music. "I swear I hear music."

"It's Onyx. She's in the bath." Zeph wanted to move the door but didn't.

Jinx closed his eyes and imagined the view. The bubbles obscured her body, running his fingers over her body. Tweaking her nipples, kissing her lips, nibbling the back of her neck, listening to her whimper and sigh during sex...feeling the heat of her body while he fucked her.

"You're thinking dirty thoughts," Zeph said. "Filthy, dirty things. I see the wheels turning in your mind."

"I am." He'd like to tug her from the bath and carry her to the bed to make love to her.

"The same things I'm probably thinking?"

"I'm sure." He had no doubt.

"I'm thinking them, too. She's a vision," Zeph said and nudged him away from the door. "She's got me thinking."

"Does she?" His best friend wasn't talking about making love to her. "Spit it out."

"What if we bought her?"

"Like a slave? She'd never go for it." He knew better.

"No." Zephyr shook his head. "We pay her debts. I figured out how much she supposedly owes and it's not nearly as much as he claims. I'm sure he's inflating it, not that it's not a pretty penny. It's small by comparison to what it could be, but he's extorting her."

"How bad?" He flexed his hands. "Couple grand?"

"Five hundred grand."

"That's a lot, but it's not five mil." They could cover it, no problem, but still. "I say we do it."

"We cover it and make Keifer think we're enchanted with her."

"We are." But he understood what was going on. "We make the ass think we're hooked and blind to what's going on, but we're the ones pulling the strings."

"Yes."

He held up his hand as the singing stopped. "But we don't tell her?" he whispered.

"Why?" Zeph directed them into the main room and away from the door. "She'll be pissed when she finds out. She'll know we lied to her."

"We're not lying to her, but if we keep it quiet for now, we'll see her true intention and interest. Plus, I want her in the dark so when Keifer tries to corner her, she's not complicit."

Zeph paced the length of the room. "No."

"No?"

"We don't have to tell her right away, you're right. But we also don't let her get that close to Keifer. No more trips to the club. She stays out of sight so we can work out the deal and even then, we don't let her go back. He's got ruthless, awful ideas for her."

"Yes, he does." Zeph stopped pacing and folded his arms. "I have some plans for her myself."

"You do?" He'd like to hear them. "Like?"

"Besides making her our girl? She's our perfect third."

He agreed one thousand percent.

"I'd like to give her time to decide if she wants that role, but I want to show her that anyone who cares about her won't care about money or what she can do for them. I want her just because she's herself."

"I couldn't agree more." He glanced over his shoulder. She remained in the bath and blew bubbles from her hand.

"She deserves to be carefree for a change," Zeph said. "And she should be able to model again, because she loves it."

Jinx nodded. He loved that notion. "I looked at her work while I was on that call with the contractors. I'm tired of dealing with those disputes, but looking at her portfolio was a lot better. She's electric in those images. An angel."

"She is gorgeous."

"Wait until I show you the other photos. You'll think even more filthy things." He'd been hard pressed not to touch himself while he'd been on the phone. He needed to relieve himself. To sink into her pussy and find completion. To feel her heat and fuck her while Zeph pumped into her ass. Or he could fuck her ass while Zeph pistoned into her pussy. He didn't care.

As long as they pleased her, he'd be happy.

"I can't wait to see them." Zeph held up his hand. "I think she's done. Want to start this relationship right?"

"By showing her gratitude and devotion by giving her the life she knows she deserves, but never expected she'd get?"

"That and by delighting in every inch of her? Yes, please."

"Then we should talk to her."

"Talk? There's so much we could be doing and I say we do it all."

"Guys?" Onyx stood before them wrapped in a towel. "You do realize I've been listening."

"For a moment," Jinx replied. He'd heard her pad up and smelled the soap on her skin. He slipped his arm around her waist. "You're hard to miss."

"Am I?" She sighed and leaned into him. "I still don't see why you're so happy to have me here."

"We have a proposition for you," Zeph said. "Not what you're expecting."

She bristled in Jinx's arms. "Whoa."

"What we're trying and failing to say is that we'd like to have you stay with us," Jinx said. "We're on to Keifer's game and the more you're not in the club, the better."

"For who?"

"All of us," Jinx said. "We want to spoil you without strings." He'd be crushed if she left, but he'd deal— after he fought like hell to win her back. She might need a few days or a few years to come around, but he was entranced by her.

"Spoil me?" she asked.

"Give us a month to show you," Zeph said. "Like Jinx said, no strings. Come and go as you like, because you'll have access to the house, the cars, able to shop if you want, and you'll get us."

"If that's something you're interested in." Jinx rubbed her bare shoulder. "I realize it's a lot to consider."

"I should say we're sweetening the pot because Jinx and I figured out Keifer's play," Zeph said.

"You did?" She sagged into Jinx. "Someone else figured it out besides me?"

"What do you believe he's doing?" Jinx asked. He let go long enough to retrieve a robe. He draped the garment around her shoulders. "You're shivering."

"Fear," she replied. "Sorry."

"Are you afraid of us?" Zeph asked. "Sweets, we're not expecting anything out of you."

"I know." She huddled against Jinx in the robe. "I'd hoped someone would see what happened and help me right the ship. If you can, then I'd be grateful."

"We will." Jinx didn't have to feign confidence, not when he saw a bully in action.

"Talk." Zephyr nodded to the bed. "Sit so you're more steady."

Jinx moved with her to the bed and sat beside her. He said nothing, but held her for support.

"Keifer offered me a way out. At first, I thought it'd be cool to work at the club because I thought he had a genuine interest and love for me. He did, but not for me personally. Not my personality or my brain. He wanted my body and what that image could do for him. How I looked. He told me after he'd paid off Nacin that I'd be good for business. Maybe I'd actually get paid. I don't know."

"In various compromising positions and play?" Jinx asked. "We saw the advertisements."

"I'd hoped they were gone, but I see they weren't destroyed." She rested her head on Jinx's shoulder, then grasped his hand. "I'm ashamed because I bought into it. I believed he cared."

"He did — about his own bottom line," Zeph said.

"But he doesn't own the club," Jinx interjected. "That's what I figured out. The manager was Darius, but the owner is a man named Xavier Norse, but it's a pseudonym for the Norse Group."

"Norse Group?" She stared at him, confusion in her eyes. "As in the people who own the magazine conglomerate?"

"A division of it." Jinx sat up straighter. "Xavier Norse is really Xavier Green. He owns a bunch of buildings in Indianapolis and oozes money. He's also a kinkster and he's been to the club a hundred times, but you'd never know it." He'd done so much digging while on the phone and loved having answers.

"Wait. What? How?" She shook her head. "I know the regulars. So does Sadie. We'd know if he was there."

"Sadie?" Zeph asked. "The redhead who came onto me the night we chose you?"

"It's black now, but I'd assume yes. She's irked you didn't choose her instead. She's salty because she wanted to run the tables and use you."

"Good thing we saw through her." Jinx grinned. He'd thought he'd sensed another charlatan in the room. "But Xavier plays as Danger."

Onyx's eyes widened. "You're kidding. Danger? He's so…"

"Timid?" Zeph asked. "Not dangerous?"

"Yes." She glanced around, no doubt trying to make sense of what she'd been told. "He's so plain. Not dangerous or even bulky."

"He's there as a sub," Jinx said. "Running the magazine division and being a businessman is tough, so his outlet is to sub at Sixxes. But so no one knows and tries to proposition him, he plays it way down low."

"I'll bet Sadie would be on him so fast if she knew." Zeph crinkled his brow. "Does it make you jealous? Change your feelings?"

"Toward you?"

"Yes," Jinx replied. "He's so sweet-natured and worth a little more than us."

"You're billionaires," she replied. "That's money I can't even imagine."

"We are, and we're going to get Keifer out of there—if it means buying out his share of the club, then that's what we'll do. We'll buy Xavier's portion or take the whole damn thing over if we have to."

"Does that mean I need to pay you back, too?" she asked.

"No." Jinx patted her butt. "Not at all."

"Oh?" Her eyes flashed. "Are you sure?"

Zeph grinned. "We don't have ill intentions for you."

"We'd like to get you back to your passion—modeling. Clothes, shoes, whatever you want. You deserve to have your career back."

"You'd do that for me?" She sagged into Jinx. "It seems so impossible."

"You'd be surprised what's possible now. You've got us in your corner," Jinx said. He refused to let her down.

Onyx couldn't believe her ears. They wanted to protect her. More than that, they were serious about keeping her and the debt would go away. "Can I make a protest?"

"Sure?" Jinx half-shrugged. "About what?"

"I want to be able to pay you back. Not just in the bedroom, but financially. I don't want to be given anything. I'm serious. I want to work for it. If I get modeling jobs, then I want to do it on my own — not because you pushed for me to have them."

"Understood." Jinx nodded. "That's fair."

"It is," Zephyr replied. "We'd like you to do some for us, though."

"Modeling?" *Probably bedroom stuff.*

"In the playroom is always a possibility, but we'd love for you to be the face of our company. The lady who owns the house in our print and media advertising. A central figure, so to speak."

"How about the spokesperson?" she asked. If she could do this collaboratively, then even better. It sounded like steady work, and respectable at that. It'd be her forte.

"That'd work." Zephyr grinned. "As long as we've got you, we want to spoil you, but we respect your boundaries."

"Agreed," Jinx added.

"But I'll assume you want me for other activities first." Those were the ones she anticipated the most. She liked being between them and she hadn't even kissed them yet.

"We do." Jinx patted her ass again. "Once we do this." He tipped her chin and caressed her jaw. His eyes lit with fire. She felt the heat and needed to be burned.

She leaned into him willingly. If she'd have known or been told he'd kiss her, much less give her this kind of attention before the night at the club, she'd never have believed it.

Now she got to experience it. His lips were softer than she expected. More demanding. The scratch of his slight stubble burned her, but she welcomed it. She opened to him right away, needing to be closer. She sucked on his tongue, tasting him for the first time. Decadent. Was that the taste of beer on his kiss? Wine? She wasn't good at differentiating the tastes. Still, she liked the way he held her and tugged her on to his lap.

The robe slipped off her shoulder and he stopped kissing her mouth to nibble along her throat, then down to her exposed skin.

"I want in on that." Zephyr settled on the other side of her. While Jinx kissed and nipped on her shoulder, Zephyr kissed her. Where Jinx started slow and built into the ferocity of the kiss, Zephyr's kiss was harder and stole her breath. She arched into him. As much as she wanted them individually, she needed them together more.

Jinx stopped the connection. "Come with us."

Zephyr parted his lips and kept his nose along hers. He tugged her to his feet. Before she could get her bearings, Zephyr scooped her into his arms. He hustled across the house.

She couldn't tell where they were going, but she didn't care. As long as she was with them, she was happy. She held tight to him.

"Better," Jinx said. He flipped on the light. "Welcome home."

Instead of being bathed in bright light, a warm yellow glow filled the room. Zephyr placed her on her feet. The robe slipped the rest of the way down her body and she abandoned the garment on the floor. The chilly air swirled around her and her nipples beaded. She loved being on display, which added to her desire.

The passion in Jinx's eyes matched the heat in Zephyr's. Jinx unbuttoned his pants first.

She hadn't been able to truly see either man and had no idea what they looked like with their clothes off, but she wasn't let down. She had the best view possible. Jinx stood before her, nude from the waist up. She got a view of his muscles and tattoos. Defined pecs and pierced nipples. How had she missed this before?

He hadn't disrobed at the club and he hadn't shown himself off.

Before she could help herself, she dropped to her knees and opened his jeans. Jinx groaned. He rested his hands on his hips, allowing her the freedom to play.

She shivered as Zephyr leaned over and kissed her shoulder. She needed to be with them. To lick, touch and taste them. When Zephyr sat back, she licked her lips.

"Want me?" Jinx asked. He threaded his fingers into her hair. "Yes, babe."

She whimpered, then wrapped her fingers around his cock. She stroked him a few times before flicking her tongue across the blunt head.

"Gods, yes." He tugged lightly on her hair. "Feels good."

She liked that. She flattened her tongue along the underside of his cock. When he moaned, she swallowed him deep. He filled her mouth and bumped the back of her throat. Being filled and controlled made her fly.

He set the pace but she didn't mind. She allowed him to push her. He sank deep into her mouth, then pulled back. When he did, she swallowed him. She buried her nose in his short curls and when she looked up at him, he smiled.

The simple gesture warmed her to her core. She moved faster, pushing herself. The more she pleased him and Zephyr, the more she freed herself.

Zephyr petted her hair. "I love this view. You're good at making him happy. Nice and wet."

She moaned around Jinx's dick. Those words from Zephyr added to her delight.

Zephyr let go and moved out of her line of sight. Damn. She wanted to look at him. Wanted to watch him while she pleased Jinx.

She heard the screech of a zipper. She wasn't sure where the sound had come from, but instead of looking, she bobbed her head. She built into a steady rhythm. She embraced the headiness of blowing him. The taste of his pre-cum on her tongue combined with the thrill of lapping at him. She swore he overwhelmed her. How in the hell was she going to handle it all?

Heat engulfed her. Her pussy tingled and she pressed her knees together. She should touch herself, but held back. She'd please herself later.

She swore she heard a whoosh, but again couldn't tell where it had come from. She continued to bob her head. Giving over this control was almost more than she could understand. He fucked her mouth harder and she groaned, happy to be on her knees. She trusted them and that they'd take care of her. Why not? They were more than she'd ever expected or deserved. They wanted her to get back to her first love, modeling, and saw her as an asset. Not a financial move, but a person who had ambitions and desires. Someone with gifts to bring to the table.

No one had ever seen her that way before. At least not that she could recall.

Hands touched her hips. "Come on. Let me see your ass."

She knew that voice. Zephyr. She immediately complied. She propped herself on her hands and knees, waggling her butt at him.

"No, girl. Use your hands on him," Zephyr said. "You know what to do."

She did. She fondled Jinx's balls in one hand and stroked him with her other hand while sucking on him. Every cell in her body screamed for him and Zephyr. She had to please them.

Zephyr stood her up enough for her to bend at the waist. She continued to blow Jinx, loving the headiness of it. At the same time, Zephyr spanked her. Not a scene, but they were certainly in control.

Zephyr spanked her a second time. "Do you want to please both of us? Girl?"

"Yes," she managed around Jinx's cock. She wanted to say more, but it was impossible. Why talk when she could enjoy the evening?

Zephyr spanked her a third time. "You're ours."

Instead of the feelings she got at the club during a scene, she truly believed she belonged to them. She was theirs through and through.

The snap of something echoed in the air. She wasn't sure what she heard, but didn't care. Zephyr spanked her inner thigh. She knew what to do and widened her stance.

"Good girl." Zephyr reached around her. He toyed with her clit. "Moan for me."

She groaned around Jinx's shaft. Her synapses misfired. She panted and met his gaze.

Before she could understand what was happening, she rocked forward. Zephyr continued to fondle her clit. He rubbed and pinched her sensitive skin. Each caress and pluck pushed her closer to coming apart. This was definitely a scene, but she wasn't sure she could let go and accept the orgasm. She wanted their approval. Wanted them to give her permission to come.

She shivered. Her brain swam as Zephyr pushed into her. Her breath lodged in her throat. He overwhelmed her. He stretched her as he pushed inside. She bore down on him, trying to adjust to the fullness in her pussy. When he touched her clit again, her knees turned to jelly.

Feelings developed and she'd never be able to deny her attraction to Zephyr and Jinx. Hell, she didn't understand how she felt yet, but she knew to her soul that she couldn't break free. She kept her thoughts to herself.

Zephyr filled her to the hilt. As he rocked forward, fucking her, she swallowed Jinx deeper. The men had control. They had her right where they wanted her, but also where she wanted to be. She allowed them to push her. To embrace every second. To love and live without barriers around her heart.

Jinx and Zephyr would protect her. She had no doubt. She basked in the good feelings. She moaned around Jinx's cock and praised Jesus that Zephyr had a hold on her. She might have collapsed from sheer pleasure otherwise.

Jinx lurched forward. "Ah, fuck. I love your mouth. You're good. Got me right at the edge."

She loved hearing that. She curled her tongue around him and swallowed.

He growled and surged into her mouth. "Oh my God." He pushed deeper. He jerked, then spilled his seed down her throat. She lapped at him, not wanting to miss a drop.

Her thoughts scattered. All she could do was ride the wave of pleasure. She rocked closer to coming. She wanted to let go, but held back.

Zephyr pushed into her harder. He bit into her hip with the fingers of his right hand. He pinched her clit with his other hand. "Want to come?"

She tried to answer, but Jinx remained in her mouth. She nodded, but didn't release her hold on Jinx's dick.

"Good girl." Zephyr pumped harder into her. The slap of skin on skin seemed so loud in the room. His growls filled the space. He swatted her while pistoning into her. "Ours."

Yes, she belonged to them. She'd keep her thoughts to herself, but she did want to be theirs. She liked being owned.

"Ours," Jinx said. He released his grasp on her hair, then petted her head. He withdrew from her mouth. "So beautiful, too. Love seeing you on my dick."

She wanted to ride his cock. Having Zephyr inside her was heaven, but she wanted both erections in her body. Wanted them stretching her. To feel the exquisite burn.

She rested her head on Jinx's lap as she embraced the orgasm building in her. She'd never felt so loved or treasured as she did in this moment. The prickles of climax grew stronger. She panted and glanced up at Jinx.

Jinx nodded slightly. "Come apart. Come with Zeph and let go."

She couldn't hold back if she tried. She tumbled right over the edge. The bliss of coming filled her head. She swore she floated. Her limbs were weightless. A sigh escaped her lips.

Zephyr slammed into her. "Christ. You're so wet. So needy. Feels so fucking good." He pushed into her faster and his movements turned feral. He cried out.

She rocked into Jinx's lap. When Zephyr pushed harder into her, she rode the new waves of pleasure.

"Fuck." Zephyr held tight to her hips. He kept his cock buried balls deep in her as he throbbed. He dug his hands into her skin. "Jesus Christ."

She sagged onto Jinx's thighs. She didn't need to think. Couldn't even if she'd have wanted to because the orgasm overwhelmed her.

Zephyr pulled out and lowered Onyx's knees to the floor.

She allowed Jinx to tug her onto his thighs and tucked her to his chest. Her eyelids were heavy. Bliss and the bone-deep weariness filled her mind. She wanted to curl up on him and never leave. She didn't mind that she was nude. Didn't care who saw her. She curled her knees to her chest.

Zephyr sank onto the bed and brushed her hair from her face. "Rest now."

Not that she'd argue.

"You've had a long day," Zephyr said. "It's time to rest and allow yourself to breathe."

"You've been told before that it's under control, but we won't do you wrong," Jinx said. "You can trust us."

She knew. She met Zephyr's gaze, but said nothing.

"We'll treat you right because you deserve it. You're a gem," Zephyr said. "We'll get this sorted out. But more than that, we'll show you that not every man is trash. You're the kind of woman who should be treasured. Not for your body or your abilities, but for your mind. For all of you."

She lifted her head. "You're serious."

"I am," Zephyr said.

"I am, too," Jinx added. "We might not tell you everything right away, but we'll never lie to you."

She trusted them. "Will you sleep with me tonight? Stay with me?"

"Of course." Jinx let go of her long enough to kick out of his pants the rest of the way. "I don't want to be anywhere else."

She crawled into the bed, between the sheets. The scent of their detergent, or maybe it was their cologne, swirled around her. When Jinx climbed in beside her, she welcomed his arm across her belly.

Zephyr stripped nude, then joined them in bed. He tangled his legs with hers. "Sleep, sweets. We've got you."

"Thank you." She kissed Jinx, then Zephyr. She closed her eyes. Her issues weren't gone. Far from it, but she had a plan and two men who were determined to give her a chance. She'd take whatever she could get.

She could handle anything because she found a place where she belonged.

Finally.

It couldn't have been more than a few seconds before she collapsed in sleep. She didn't dream. The blessed darkness swallowed her and she could rest.

Chapter Six

Onyx cuddled between her men and sighed as she woke. For once, she was safe and comfortable. She saw promise in the future. She could work and enjoy herself. Could be her own woman.

Her phone beeped. No, it rang in the irritating tone belonging to the club. *Fuck.* She nearly jumped out of her skin. She didn't want to answer it and have this moment end. She also didn't want Zephyr and Jinx to hear the blasted device.

"Why do I hear a ringer like the ones at Sixxes?" Jinx asked. "And why do I hear it at this time of the morning?"

She swore she blushed from head to toe. Why couldn't the phone stop ringing so she could claim it was a dream or they'd misheard the noise?

"Why is it still ringing?" Zephyr asked. "I hate being woken up by a phone."

She couldn't hide any longer. "Sorry. It's mine." She wanted to melt into the floor. She scrambled out of bed, then froze. "I hear it, but I don't know where it's at." She'd have to learn the layout of the home soon because failing wasn't an option. She had to show them she had brains.

Besides, she wanted to ignore her phone. If the ringtone for the club was blasting, then it had to be because Keifer wanted her attention. If that was the case, then it had to be because he had something for her to do. Or he'd caught wind of her taking off with Zephyr and Jinx. If he knew that, then he'd want in on the potential financial windfall.

The faster he forgot she existed, the happier she'd be.

"Let me get you something to wear and show you where to find the phone." Zephyr left the bed. He strode nude across the room to the closet. "Here." He withdrew a bright white dress shirt.

She accepted the garment. "Thanks," she muttered. She'd have to bring her clothes to the house. Not that she wanted them to see her bland wardrobe.

"A woman looks better in a man's shirt than a man could ever appear. At least, that's what I believe." Zephyr offered his hand. "It's a big house and we never did give you the tour." He led her from the room while Jinx remained in bed.

"What about Jinx? He's not coming?" He wasn't going to witness her embarrassment?

"He needs a little more time to wake up." Zephyr chuckled and laced his fingers with hers. "Wake him too fast and without coffee…you're in for a fight."

"Oh." She'd have to do something about that.

"I'm used to it." He walked with her down the hallway. "We had a girl who made coffee for him, but she got tired of being here."

She stopped in her tracks. Knowing they had someone else shouldn't have shocked her. It was natural. Still, the knowledge stunned her. "Is she still here?" She hadn't even looked at the surroundings or anything along the way. He consumed her entire attention. "If you have someone else, I'm out."

"Whoa." He kept hold of her hand, albeit gingerly, but didn't stop walking. "You misunderstand me. She was the cleaner."

She should've guessed they'd have some sort of staff.

"She wanted to be more than one of the help, so to speak, and thought if she catered to our every whim, we'd marry her."

"You didn't?" she blurted.

"Nope. I've never been married. Forty-six years old and still a bachelor," Zephyr said proudly. "I've been called horrible, but I'm not above waiting until I get exactly what I want."

"That makes sense, but why not marry her? She did what you wanted and I'm guessing she did it almost before you knew she wanted it." It all seemed correct—and also made her want to tamp down her desire to be with them. She could be tossed aside, too.

"She did what we wanted and some of what she wanted, but it wasn't her true motivation. There's a big difference in being something for someone else and being yourself." He tugged her down to the kitchen. When he walked in, he tapped a pad on the wall, illuminating the smart screen. The lights turned fully on and the coffee pot switched on.

"The idea of the cleaner or girl Friday is to be what you want and to do what you want," she said. "It's your house and she should do your bidding."

"Correct. I do have exacting standards, but I like my partners to have their own free will and express themselves. That's why Jinx and I are friends. We're a lot alike, but very different at the same time. I play off his challenges to me because I need it. He's impulsive and I'm a planner. Sometimes you need to plan and others you need to be impulsive, so we balance each other."

"So that's what made her too much of what you wanted?" She didn't understand.

"What if she didn't want to make the coffee each morning, but she did it to make us happy? What if she waited on us hand and foot, but we weren't interested? Not for every second? She thought she knew what we wanted, but she didn't have a clue. She wanted to be Mrs. Collins and had determination, which was great, but she had an odd way of showing it. I knew exactly what she truly wanted beyond marriage. She wanted the access to our money and social standing. She wanted the perceived perks."

Her mind swam with information. "Wait."

"There are perks in being with us, I won't lie. We'll spoil you rotten and will show you how you're cherished and loved. You'll know how much we care. At any second, if you doubt our feelings, we'll tell you. Show you. You'll have our full love and respect. But we expect that in return."

"That makes sense." She settled on a stool. "Did she push?"

"So hard." He pulled three cups from the cabinet. "She thought she'd be smart and suck up to us. She tried to give gifts and her submission."

"Oh, so you played with her." She didn't want to share them with anyone.

"Not really." He turned off the coffee machine and poured the brew into the three cups. He offered her one. "Jinx will join us in a moment. I'm sure he's caught a whiff of the coffee by now."

"Oh, okay." She wrapped her hands around the cup.

"Cream? Sugar?" He pulled a container from the fridge.

"Cream, please." She accepted the container. She's almost missed the doors of the fridge, mistaking them for just another set of doors in the cabinets. "Thank you." She poured a bit of the cream into her cup.

"No problem." He toyed with his cup. "Before we get further along, we need to be clear."

"Right." She should've guessed. He'd lower the boom now. "I'm listening."

"I hope so." He waited for Jinx to shuffle into the room. "Morning, gorgeous George."

Jinx scrubbed his hand through his short hair. "Sorry." He sank onto the stool next to hers and grabbed the cream without another word.

"Hi." She tensed in her seat. "I'm glad you're awake. He was going to get serious."

"Oh." Jinx dumped more cream into his cup, then a generous helping of sugar. "Serious? So early?"

"Yes." Zephyr stood across from them at the counter. "I believe a little clarification is needed."

"Sure. I follow." Jinx sipped his coffee. "I need a spoon, my good man."

Zephyr offered up two spoons. "Sorry. I just let mine mix as the cup moves. I forget others want to stir theirs."

"So what are we getting serious about?" she asked.

"Desiree." Zephyr leaned his elbows on the counter. "And her position in the house."

She wished she understood, but she wasn't about to ask any other questions. She stirred her coffee as it mixed and cooled.

"The clarification is that she pushed to get what she wanted by trying to be what she thought we requested. Her greed was her true driving force. Money, status," Zephyr said. "She'd have put up with our lifestyle, but that's just it. Putting up with it isn't enjoying it. The cash is good, but if there's no real emotion behind it, then we're not giving it out. We're not interested in someone who doesn't have their heart in the relationship."

It all made so much more sense now. "You don't think that's what I might be after?"

"I know you're not after that because you're different.," Jinx said. "Very different."

"I know you are, too," Zephyr said. "You had a career and life. You'd made your own way and had your own things going. You did it before and can do that again with a little help. You don't need our money or status. Not when you had your own. You're cunning and clever, but you're smart. You've got heart, too. Once you get going, it'll be easier."

Not exactly easy. She'd been out of the game for too long. "It might not be what you think."

"You can do it," Zephyr said. "The debt is just a roadblock."

"It is." *A monumental one.*

"But Desiree's issue was her greed. I won't marry anyone who only wants me for my money," Jinx said. "Neither will Zeph. We've seen too many people ruined because they connected with a con."

"And she was a con," Zephyr said. "She'd have been happy, but would we? No."

"How do you know though, that I'm not like her? You barely know me." She had to dissuade them, even if only to save herself. She'd fallen for them and needed to protect herself. "I could be just as bad."

"You could, but we know you're not," Jinx said. "Trust us."

She'd love to and she had the feeling they'd be good to her — but did she deserve it?

"There are tells and we know what they are," Zephyr said. "Not that we'd tell you. You're fine. Just please believe us."

"Why are you so hard to resist?" She stared at them. "I'm not perfect. Barely even good, but I'd like the chance to be with you." She wasn't sure why she'd felt she had to say those things.

"Consider it done." Jinx winked. "Besides, we're not letting go easily."

"We don't." Zephyr sipped his coffee. "So would you like us to have the car brought somewhere?"

"Towed?" *Great.* She'd end up with another hole in the oil pan. "Better not."

"Flat bedded," Zephyr replied. "We're going to let Keifer think we're taking it as collateral. Keep up the ruse that you're now into us for that cash and we're finding ways to take it out of your ass."

She hated the way it sounded, but she agreed. "Just as long as the oil pan doesn't get pierced. It always does when it's towed."

"How many times have you had to have that done?" Jinx asked.

"I got a flat tire that shredded on the rear left and when they towed it, the towing company put a hole in the pan. Then I was front ended and the same thing happened. Seems like a trend."

"What'd you run over?" Zephyr asked. "You don't just shred a tire."

She flicked her gaze from one man to the other. She hated talking about her life, but they should know. "I have horrible luck sometimes. Like with the tires. I didn't know I'd gone over the wrong side of the exit. I went the way I was told and managed to shred the tire. The crash wasn't my fault. The guy said he didn't see me and backed into me. But it's like other things. Nacin could've targeted so many other girls, but he chose me. I could've been saved the pain, but I was targeted." She hadn't realized she harbored so much anger still.

"Whoa." Zephyr rounded the counter and embraced her. "Slow down."

She hadn't realized she was shaking. "Sorry."

"I get that you're frustrated and scared, but Nacin won't hurt you," Zephyr said. "He can try, but he'll fail."

"I know." She trusted them that much.

"I can't say what the true motivation was with the tire," Jinx said. "But it's possible you were told the wrong side to be destructive and someone being an intentional dick. That said, it's also remotely possible that it was a simple misunderstanding. I doubt it, though."

So did she.

"That doesn't mean you have terrible luck, though." Zephyr cupped her jaw in both hands. "To be honest, Nacin chose the best girl—hear me out—trust me."

Why did that sound so terrible? She kept quiet, instead of arguing.

"He chose the woman who is strong, tenacious and sure, she's scared, but she stood up to him. He expected to get his way and expected you to give right in, but you didn't. You've been a thorn in his side, you know. You didn't give up and that upsets him."

"I hid."

"That doesn't matter. You had to heal." Zephyr continued to caress her cheek. "He chose someone who wouldn't back down. Many other people would've collapsed. You stood tall."

Technically, he was right, but it didn't feel correct.

"You don't trust what you've accomplished. You're a gem. Not perfect, but who is?" Zephyr asked.

"You," she murmured.

"Nope. Ask Jinx. I'm not perfect. I think too much, too hard, and consider things for too long when I'm making choices. I get too hung up on my appearance and work too hard to ensure I look like this."

"I never feel I look good enough," Jinx said. "Always convinced I've got pencil on my face from a drawing or graphite on my hands which I then smear somewhere embarrassing. I'm not a ladies' man like I've been told I should be. I'm reminded I have some cash and I should be stronger, harsher and concerned less about what others think. I should be myself and it's hard."

"It is." She admired his honesty.

"But what we're trying to say is that he could've chosen anyone else, but he chose a woman he couldn't quite control. His mistake," Zephyr said. "It's hard to believe me, but we wouldn't lie about this."

She held onto his wrists. "I know." He made a good point.

"We need to work today, but we're going to have your car towed out," Jinx said. "Then we're going to get some of our own work done."

"Will you be all right on your own?" Zephyr asked. "You've got access to the cars or we can have a driver take you around."

She'd have to figure out what she wanted to do, but she liked the freedom. "Thanks. I'll be fine. I'm not sure what I'll do today, but I appreciate the belief in me."

Jinx winked. "You deserve it."

"Thanks." She wriggled free from Zephyr. "Do what you need to do. I'm not here to be a problem." She'd leave if she was a bother.

"Never." Zephyr grabbed his coffee. "We do need to get work done. At least check in with the contractors and managers."

She agreed. They couldn't change their life around for her. "I have a request, if it's not too much."

"Oh?" Jinx remained in his seat. He held onto his cup. "Expense account? Credit card?"

"Own car?" Zephyr asked. "A ring? Collar?"

"No. No." They were quick to believe she was so materialistic. "I'd like a room to myself. The room I stayed in? I'd like to keep it to sort out my belongings. You can search the room at any time, but I'd like a space of my own." She refused to keep secrets.

"Who says we're checking on you?" Zephyr asked. "I should be offended."

"I've seen the cameras all over," she said. "They're hard to miss."

"No, but they're not to keep an eye on you," Jinx said. "Sometimes you've got to protect your kingdom."

"We've worked hard to get the house how we want and so forth, but when you don't do something to a customer's standards, they tend to get cranky. Some get really worked up." Zephyr refreshed his coffee. "We've been lucky, but you never know."

"No." She understood exactly what he meant. She lived in the constant fear Keifer would retaliate or Nacin would opt to follow through on his threats. The last thing she wanted was to lose her freedom because of someone's arrogance.

"We've got to handle meetings today, but we can get you where you want to go. We've got drivers if you'd like," Jinx said, then dumped the coffee into the sink.

"I'd like that." First, she needed to return to her phone and figure out what Keifer wanted. She wasn't scheduled to be at the club until four, but she doubted she'd be there again. "I'd like a shower first, then I'd like to go out."

"Sure." Zephyr hesitated. "We've got a dinner tonight. It's an award for philanthropy."

"You're philanthropists, too?" What weren't they involved in? They were almost too good to be true. And they wanted her? She seriously wondered how they weren't snapped up yet.

"We've given money to a few causes," Jinx said. "Help those who can't help themselves and be kind."

"You're unbelievable." She shook her head. "I don't get why you've been single for so long."

"We were waiting for the right partner." Zephyr's eyes flashed. "Think we've found her?"

"Maybe." She wasn't about to disagree. But that was her problem. She tended not to argue and stand up for herself.

Jinx elbowed Zephyr. "I'd love to stay here all day and be together, but I have a design meeting at ten."

Was it that late already? She shifted in her seat. "Go. I'll be fine."

"Never doubted that." Jinx kissed her. "Tonight, you have my full attention."

"I look forward to it." *Truly.*

Jinx left the room, but Zephyr remained.

She eyed him. "Am I in trouble?"

"No, but I have to get you out of that mindset. You're not a bad girl."

"But I could be."

"You are at times, but not now." His eyes glittered. "Relax. We're not here to cage you. This is freedom."

She nodded.

"I need to speak to marketing with my ideas. Expect a call from them to discuss them with you." Zephyr kissed her and lingered a moment. "You're part of the team, but you're mostly part of our family now. We're with you. Remember that."

"I will."

"Enjoy yourself today," he said. "I'll handle Keifer."

On that account, she trusted them completely. "Thank you."

"Enjoy yourself," he repeated. "I'll find you later."

"Thank you."

Chapter Seven

As Zephyr left the room, Onyx considered the circumstances and her choices. Luck wasn't her friend. Most of the time, things went her way out of sheer determination, but she didn't stand up for herself much, especially in relationships. When she had, she'd been hurt. She equated being bold with being hurt. Men tended to want demure women. She wasn't demure, but she'd learned to be that way. She'd learned through her modeling to pack away her emotions. She'd done the same thing in relationships.

Except with Nacin.

That was the one time she'd screamed and he'd treated her like shit.

This wasn't the first instance she'd pushed her feelings down. She'd done it when she was a child and has been teased for being tall and thin. She'd done it when she'd been in high school to hide the fact she didn't like being the breadwinner for her family. She'd buried her heart when she'd started baring her body.

When she'd done a scene or modeled kink wear, she'd been more able to show her emotions. Stripping down freed her. Then again, so did the scenes. She could show emotions but pretend she was someone else. No one could hurt her then.

It was odd. The pain in the scenes didn't bother her, but being bold and pushy always created an ache. The scenes gave her freedom.

She made her way to the suite. Once in the doorway, she stopped to drink in her surroundings. The place was lush. With thick carpets and heavy drapes, the room looked like a professional had decorated it. No dust. Nothing out of order. Like the room was never used.

Shouldn't it have been?

She opened the cupboards and drawers. Everything was solid wood and well-built. The curtains were actual cotton, not something synthetic. Soft, too.

She snorted. She'd modeled with furnishings quite similar for a campaign revolving around perfume. It was an odd setting for a perfume shoot, but the idea was that people of taste used that scent. Did they? She wasn't sure.

But she'd been the face of the campaign. Moira Jones, another model, had been the brand ambassador and new fresher face of the campaign. Fine by Onyx. Moira needed the attention more.

She sat on the bed and stared at the bureau. Did she belong in the fancy house? With these guys?

Yes. She sat up straighter. She did deserve it because she deserved to be happy. She'd given up a lot in her life and should have something good.

She also wanted her job back. To be responsible for herself, which wasn't too much to ask.

She headed to the shower and turned on the water. She stripped out of the shirt as the steam billowed in the room. The space was clean and spartan, practically sparkling—like she hadn't used it earlier. She guessed they had people to clean, but she had no idea when they'd come in. Not that it mattered right now.

She stepped into the shower. The hot spray stung her body. As much as she wanted to luxuriate in the water, she wanted to start her life on a better track.

She washed and conditioned her hair, then cleansed her body before rinsing. Once finished, she turned off the water and left the stall. She'd posed in some fancy bathrooms—once for a shaving cream ad and once for a lingerie shoot, but this space was the best. There were good acoustics, plenty of natural light and great ventilation. Even the floor was warm. She dried her hair, then rushed out to the bedroom and her bag. She tucked the towel around her body as she checked her phone. The screen flashed.

Shit. She'd forgotten all about the earlier call. She picked up the device. The screen lit again with the notifications of at least seven missed calls and more than forty messages. She groaned. The man had no patience.

She entered the code for her voicemail and tapped the first message.

"I saw you left last night. Saw who you left with, too. Hope you're working a deal." He hung up, but she knew the venom in his voice.

She tapped the last voicemail. She might as well listen to the finality of it all. He was angry and her car might not even be there. It might be in a compactor.

"Called your new friends and left a message. Must be blowing them. Good. Keep them happy. I expect you to scratch my back on this one. You owe me, remember? If you want your car and your belongings here at the club, then you'll have to cooperate. Got it?" He hung up again, leaving her in shocked silence.

The asshole.

"Onyx."

She wiped her face, then glanced up from the phone. Zephyr stood in the doorway. "Hi." She didn't have to say more. She knew in her gut that he'd heard the messages.

"What—no." Zephyr strode into the room. "I heard him. I came down here because I got a similar message. He's expecting us to pay up so you can be ours. How do you feel about that?"

"Shitty." There was no point in mincing words. "He's trying to con."

"We know."

"And using me." *Again.* "Do you have suggestions for what I should do? I'm not ruling anything out."

"I told you we'd take care of you."

"You did."

"Also said we'd handle this."

"You did." She wasn't a fan of having these kinds of conversations in the nearly nude, but whatever. "Might I add that I'm not wild about being pushed around?" *Outside of a scene.*

"You may and I appreciate it." He settled next to her. "May I listen to the rest of the messages?"

"Sure." There was no point in hiding. She offered him the phone. "It's unlocked. Tap here to listen to them and the texts are here." She pointed to the app.

He accepted the device and switched it from the speaker setting. As he listened to each message, the creases in his forehead deepened. He gritted his teeth and a growl rose from his throat.

She winced. Men who growled like that, or kept a lid on their anger in this manner, scared her because the lid could blow at any second and that anger be directed at her.

"Sweetheart, you're not at fault." He lowered the phone. "This ass is bent on trouble. It's his type."

"But you're angry." And that's what bothered her.

"I am, but not at you. I can tell it's freaking you out that I'm irked and I'm sorry. I didn't mean to scare you."

"I know."

"Can you believe me we'll handle this?" Zephyr asked. "Can you?"

"I can."

"Try to relax and enjoy yourself here. We'll make you feel like a queen if you'll give us the chance. Take yourself out and buy a dress for the dinner. It's a banquet, so think formal. A cocktail dress." He tapped information into her phone. "Go to Laurello's and ask for Erin. She'll take care of you. Promise."

"Okay." She leaned into his embrace. "I'm afraid of him, but I trust you. I can't wait to go out tonight and have a good time. I know we will."

"We will."

Hers was a pretty big change in attitude, but living in the past and kicking herself was getting old fast. Why not embrace the new? She'd get to go shopping today and allow herself to be spoiled. Who didn't want to be treated like a princess? "I know you will."

Zephyr kissed her, then stood. "I really do need to get to work. I'd rather be here with you." He didn't like leaving her this way. She'd been through so much and used even more.

Right now, he had to get something accomplished and it wasn't work.

"You'll be okay?" he asked. He lingered in the doorway again. "Sweetheart?"

"I will." She smiled and for the first time since she'd entered the house, the smile seemed real. The light in her eyes added to her beauty. She didn't look tired or weathered, as she had at the club, but fresh and happy. Younger. She finally looked her twenty-eight years and he loved that about her. Loved it *for* her. She continued to grin, then blushed.

"What?" he asked.

"I was going to ask you that. You're staring at me in an odd way. Like you're seeing me for the first time," she said. "Forgot who I was?"

"Nah." He winked. "In a way, I am seeing you for the first time and you've got me attracted." More than attracted. He wanted to fuck her right now. That'll have to wait.

"Good." She blushed deeper red. "I'll see Erin and have one of your…people…drive me there?"

"You should. I let her know you'd be heading there at some point." He debated staying with her, but instead, he walked away from the door.

Zephyr forced himself down the hall to the other side of the house. He snatched his phone from his desk and squeezed the device. How dare Keifer treat her like shit? Demand money. The nerve of the guy.

He snapped his fingers.

A moment he did, Jinx opened the door between the offices. "You summoned me?"

He hated when Jinx said that. "Sorry. I wanted to get your attention."

"You've got it." Jinx folded his arms. "What's up? She's okay? I should've gone back to the room and checked on her."

"I did and she's okay. Shaken, but okay."

"Shaken?" Jinx stood taller. "How so? What happened?"

"Long story short, Keifer was the jackass texting and calling her."

"He's the reason we were woken up this morning," Jinx said. "We assumed that was the case."

"And we were right. He also texted me, too. Called and I didn't answer because we were doing something more important," Zephyr said. "I don't want to talk to the ass anyway."

"What did he do, though? He had to have said something." Jinx shook his head. "If you're pissed and she's upset, then this isn't a good thing."

"It's not. He did his best sweet talk to get us to pay a little more for her and maybe kick in for a few other things," Zephyr said. "Which...whatever. He's not getting what he thinks, but I'm not arguing with him right now. It's what he said to her that has me livid. The jackass told her he might not have her car there if he decides to have it removed. He might hold her things hostage, too. Why should he let her have her stuff if she's not playing along and working a little harder to land the big fish? That's what he sees us as, big fish he can net and she's the bait."

"Fucker."

"That's one way of putting it." He sank onto the leading edge of his desk. "Thing is, I'm going to fuck with him. Did you get her car towed?"

"Flat bedded about ten minutes ago. I saw them put it on the truck," Jinx said. "So he can't say that."

"Can if he wants to scare her." At least he knew his best friend had the car situation under control. That relieved him. "But, he wants her there tonight. Either come in, or serve you and I up on a silver platter."

"Jesus."

"I know."

"Call the bastard out."

"I plan on it, but I want to toy with him. I'm going to call him, but I wanted you to be around to hear the call. I don't trust him and we're in this together." He produced his phone and dialed the club. He should've had the direct number to Keifer, but he wanted to go through the proper channels. After three rings, the call connected.

"Hello?" a female voice said. "This is Sixxes. We're here to make your dreams and kinkiest desires come true. How may I direct your call?"

"Hello, may I ask who I'm speaking to?" Zephyr switched the call to speaker.

"This is Sadie. How can I help you?"

Ah, so she was the famous Sadie. "I'm looking for Keifer. He phoned me this morning, but I don't have his number to return the call."

"Then may I ask who is calling? So I can let him know?" Sadie asked. "He's in his office."

Probably decorated with whips, chains and photos of the subs. "This is Zephyr Anderson."

"Oh my God. You're…yes. I'll get him. Holy shit." Sadie moved the phone, causing static and a scratching sound.

Jinx rolled his eyes. He grabbed a piece of paper from the desk and wrote *unprofessional* on it. Zephyr had to agree, but he guessed her reaction was truer than she wanted to admit.

The scratching stopped and the line cleared. "Just a moment for Mr. Jones. Here you go."

He sighed and waited for Keifer. Good thing he wasn't holding onto the phone or he would've thrown it. The bullshit formalities annoyed him.

"Mr. Anderson," Keifer said. "It's good to hear from you. I'd hoped you'd phone me today. How are you?"

"Fine. You?" He hated sleazy people and Keifer dripped with scum.

"I'm wonderful."

Right. He pinched the bridge of his nose. "You called me, but the message was garbled and I couldn't make out what you'd said. Did you want to speak with me?"

Jinx massaged his temples.

"I did," Keifer replied. "I'm sorry the message was garbled. I thought it was pretty clear. Guess my end of the line was messed up."

"That happens. Phones don't always work right."

"No, they don't," Keifer said. "What I called about concerns a woman you played with at the club. I don't know how closely you read the rules and fine print."

"Quite closely. I don't get into deals without reading them." He picked at lint on his shirt. "She's a house slave, yes. I also read that house slaves can't be released without proper payment. I'm assuming this call has to do with that payment, or the request for such funds."

"I—yes."

He liked having Keifer off his guard. "So? What did you want to discuss?"

"She left with you and your partner last night. Being that she's a house slave, she's indebted to the club and the house. I don't know if she's mentioned those debts."

"She has."

"Ah, good. Sob story? She's good for those. Likes to make people think she's in trouble when she's not. You'll figure that out, but I thought I'd save you some time," Keifer said. "But if you want to know how much she's into me for, it's about three quarters of a mil."

Interesting. He'd looked into the figures and it wasn't that high. "Huh. She told us it was closer to a full mil." He'd spoken out of his ass, but he didn't care. Jinx snorted and muffled the sound behind his hand. Zephyr shrugged. "So you're trying to talk us out of possibly taking her on?" He'd love to hear this answer.

"Just trying to save you the hassle of getting taken," Keifer said. "But if you're interested in her, she's a hard worker. Just an exaggerator."

"We've noticed that," Zephyr said. He might as well see how much rope Keifer would take before making an ass of himself. "She mentioned something about Nacin."

"Yeah, that's a crock of shit, too," Keifer replied. "She says he assaulted her and she talks a good game. Makes it really feel like something happened, but I know Nacin. He's not that kind of guy. If he wants a woman, he gets her. Doesn't have to stoop to chasing someone who isn't interested. She didn't like that he turned her down and she expected special favors from him, but when he didn't do it, she claimed he'd treated her poorly."

Zephyr nearly swallowed his tongue. *Treated her poorly? Good God.* He'd love to know what Keifer considered kind treatment. *She didn't like being turned down?* He scrubbed his forehead with the back of his hand. He'd done his due diligence with the stories she'd told and the news that had come out concerning

Nacin. Nothing he'd read made him believe she was lying. Not a thing.

"She can be a troublemaker, but she's worth it," Keifer said. "You should make a play for her."

He met Jinx's gaze and crooked his brow. "How about we keep her a while and see if she changes her story? In the meantime, we'll kick in half a mil to buy that time. Yeah?" He let the words hang there, expecting Keifer to accept.

He could practically hear the salivation in Keifer's words. "That would be fine. I'll grant her a few weeks of leave for you to decide if you'd like to draw up a contract with her or you'd like to have her return to the club."

"Fine." Before Keifer could reply, Zephyr hung up. He didn't give a shit about where to send the money or if he'd even bother to wire it to the club. He'd bought them time and proven Keifer's greed.

"I guess we sort of own her?" Jinx asked. "I don't like the way it shook out, but at least she's free for now."

"She's free and she's not going back there ever." Not if he had anything to say about it. He exhaled. "I've got a campaign to start with her in it and I want you to help with the art."

"First, we've got that dinner tonight," Jinx said. "Is she getting ready?"

"I let Erin know she'll be coming to the boutique. She'll make sure Onyx is ready and even more beautiful for the event."

"And we'll give her one of a series of nights she won't forget," Jinx said. "Then we nail his ass to the wall."

"Correct." They'd not only nail Keifer's ass, but his balls, dick and everything else of value. "We protect our own and she's ours."

No question.

Chapter Eight

Jinx returned to his office and strode up to his desk. Anger bubbled in him. How dare Keifer be so cruel? Easy. The man was trash. Jinx swiped his arm across his desk, sending papers sailing through the air to the floor. He didn't want to clean up the mess, but damn it, he hated being played and Keifer was trying to run a con on him and Zeph.

He massaged his temples, then scrubbed the back of his hand across his forehead. He'd rather be creating right now. His phone buzzed and he sighed. Now who wanted him?

He swiped to check the notification. A text from Zeph.

I've got K in hand. Sent an email with my ideas – rough – for the print media. See what you can do with it.

He didn't need to reply. He'd been given a challenge and he couldn't wait to tackle it. Zeph was the businessman. Zeph knew how to work deals and handle money. He could be absolutely dangerous when given a project to price out. He knew where to cut corners and when to go more expensive, while keeping the project at a good rate.

Jinx didn't like numbers. He lived for the art and colors. He opened the email and read through the bulleted list. Every one of the suggestions involved Onyx.

Perfect. He could see the exact vision Zeph had and knew how he wanted to bring it to fruition. But he didn't want to sketch the images. He'd rather do some photos. The only way to do that would be to talk to Onyx.

No time like now. Hell, he could go with her to the stores and keep her company.

He rushed across the house to the guest suite, then knocked on her door. "Onyx?"

"Yes?" She yanked the door open. She wore a simple long-sleeve blouse and jeans, no shoes or socks, and her hair was pulled back in a ponytail. A few wisps of hair curled around her face. She hadn't put on any makeup, but her cheeks were stained pink. "Hi."

"Hi. May I come in?"

She frowned for a split-second, then grinned. "It's your house."

"But this is your space." He wanted to gather her in his arms and kiss her senseless, but waited for her permission.

"I guess so." She stepped out of the way. "Come in, you goof. Of course you can come in here. Are you done with your meetings?"

"Not exactly, but I need your advice on a few projects." He crossed the threshold into her suite and noticed she'd kept her belongings in her bag. Nothing was out, like a lived-in room. He couldn't wait until she felt comfortable enough to relax.

"Oh?" She pulled a pair of socks from her bag. "I didn't pack much, but I'd like to cover my feet. I'm not fond of them."

"Really?" He sat beside her and gazed at the floor. She had pretty feet. With the right pedicure, she'd be model ready, but even without, she was fine. He toyed with a lock of her hair as she bent over. "They're adorable."

"Tell that to the people who took the photos and insisted I wear pumps so they didn't stick out." She put the socks on, then sat up. "Better. I hate having cold feet."

"I get that." He studied her. She wouldn't need much makeup to be the average housewife for the print images, but she could wear something more sophisticated for the spokeswoman role.

"You're staring at me." She crooked her brow. "Now what?"

"I might as well get to the point. I'd like your collaboration on the print media campaigns and the digital ones. They aren't going to be the same, so all input is welcome."

"Oh?" She crossed her ankles and rested her hands on her lap. "I'm game."

"I hear you're going shopping. He got you in with Erin?" he asked. "Mind if I come along and we can discuss during the ride?"

"I'd love that." She brightened. "I wasn't sure how to ask someone to get me keys or to drive me."

"Then why don't I escort you?" He stood and offered his arm. "We can take the truck."

"Sounds like fun. Is Zephyr coming along?"

"No. He's busy."

"Oh." She stepped into her sneakers. "With my issues?"

He shook his head. She was too smart and observant for her own good. "Among other things. He's been sending me ideas for the media campaigns and it's time I got on them." Besides, he wanted to be creative.

"I don't know what you're planning, but I'm game. As for the other, I'm still worried, but I'll tamp it down." She picked up her purse. "I'm ready."

"Then let's go." He led her through the house to the garage to the truck. "When we bought this truck, I advocated pretty hardcore. We didn't need a truck, but it worked for the image we were trying to promote and it's fun as hell to drive." He opened the passenger door for her.

"Thank you." She hurried past him and climbed onto the seat.

Once she was settled, he closed the door, then rounded the tailgate to the driver's side. He scooted behind the wheel.

"So what are these ideas?" she asked as he backed out of the garage stall. Light bathed the truck and she folded her hands on her lap. "What direction does he want to go?"

"Well." He drove away from the house toward the main road. "So, I've got the bones of an idea from Zeph, but what I want to do is photograph you around the staging home, watching the work being done, enjoying the grass, by the planters and on the porch in the swing. Just a homeowner enjoying the work that's been done."

She toyed with her purse. "I like it. Simple and gets to the point."

"And shows off our work."

"Do you have an actual staging home?" She shifted in her seat and watched him. "A place to do this?"

"We do." He pulled onto the freeway, then into traffic. "It's our first home."

"You have another house?"

"I know it's not normal, but we kept it because we thought maybe the partnership would fracture and we'd want separate places. Thought it'd be a good idea to keep the property in case we needed it. We haven't, but it's nice to have the insurance." He'd never had to explain this before, but no one had ever asked.

"I get it. I thought I'd be smart and have a few little insurances in case I fucked stuff up, but those were depleted."

"That happens." He followed the divided highway around the city to the upper west side. The boutiques and specialty shops were all located there. So were the bigger homes with the lawns requiring more specialized work. "We kept the house and have it set up for photos or for videos. The property is big enough that we can shoot from a couple different spots and it looks like multiple locations."

"That's handy." She nodded. "Like having your own studio without actually having one."

"Exactly. It helps to have a property where family can visit and stay without being under foot, where we can entertain clients without bringing them to the house and where we can take those photos and whatnot." He eased over to the exit and left the freeway. "Zeph's mom used to love to visit and insisted she stayed there because she liked the space and privacy."

"Does she still visit?"

"No." He wasn't sure how to explain this. "She passed a couple years ago."

"I'm sorry to hear that. What about your mother? Do your parents visit? What about his dad?" She sighed and shook her head. "I shouldn't ask so many questions."

"It's fine." He stopped at the traffic light. "I don't speak to my parents because they weren't fans of my choice of career."

"Really? You're rich, handsome and self-made. Why wouldn't they like that?"

"You'd be surprised, but they wanted me to get into law. I'm not lawyer material. I love to read, but I don't want to have to study. I like art, drawing and photography. Dad felt it was a fool's errand to pursue art and Mom thinks I simply mow lawns." He pulled away from the light, then drove down the street to the lot behind the specialty shops. "It doesn't bother me, but it's aggravating that they don't respect what I've built."

"Yeah." She remained in her seat as he parked. "But I get it. My mom didn't respect what I was doing. She saw my jobs as a means to pay for her life. She spent the money I'd made until I turned eighteen and expected me to bankroll her future."

"Do you give her money?" It wasn't his business, but it'd help him understand her better.

"No, but I don't have any to give her, even if I wanted to."

"Do you want to?"

"No. She spent what I made to the tune of almost a million and a half. It took me a long time to understand what kind of money I'd made and even longer to come to terms with the fact she'd stolen it."

"You don't have to worry about that from now on." He parked in the spot and switched off the engine. "How about we go inside?"

"First, tell me what I'm doing. I'm going to be the person in the photos?"

"Yes." He unbuckled his belt. "You'd be the homeowner, in a few different outfits and with your hair done a little differently—maybe a wig or something, if you feel comfortable—to make them all unique, and taken from different angles, but yeah. You'd be the focal point person."

She nodded, then uncrossed her ankles. "I'll find outfits to wear."

"I'm sure you will." He wasn't worried about it. She'd be fine no matter what she chose to wear. "But I expect you'll have better ideas than I will as to what the images should look like. You know what lighting to use more than I do and such things."

"I haven't been in the game for a long time, but I remember a few things."

He left the truck, then rounded the hood and opened the passenger door for her. "I'm sure it'll all come back to you." Every time he wondered if he'd lost his ability to draw or his eye for creativity was starting to fizzle, he was challenged to use the abilities again and proved he could. He offered his hand. "Ready?"

"Yes." She grasped his fingers and walked with him into the boutique. "Whoa." The swell of deep red surrounded her. Plush chairs and thick carpets, gold cord and even fringe. Heavy wood and soft music. The sheer size of the rom, along with the fact that she half expected a handful of burlesque dancers to pop out from behind one of the curtains, both shocked and amazed her. The place was certainly memorable. She wasn't even sure the store was a store, but rather someone's house. A plush house and almost impossibly chic, but still someone could live there.

"Yeah, Erin likes to keep the place posh." Jinx slipped his hand along her lower back. "She loves red."

"I can tell." Her heart hammered. She'd been in plenty of stores that oozed with class, but this one overwhelmed her. She flattened her palms on her thighs to hide the shaking. She could stand nearly naked in front of other people, but being in this establishment freaked her out. "Sorry."

"You're fine," Jinx whispered. "It's a lot to take in."

She knew damn well how he'd figured out her panic, but that didn't make it any less frustrating. "Thanks. I'm still sorry."

"Don't be. I know you're stressed." He rubbed her back. "Now, where's Erin? Miss Erin?"

A woman with flame red hair, wearing a black business suit trimmed in red piping, stepped out from behind one of the curtains. Her blood-red pumps hardly made a sound on the floor. She wore just enough makeup to be pretty without going overboard. Onyx wondered if she was a model or had been at one time. The woman smiled. "Hello, Jinx. I haven't seen you in here in a long time. How have you been and where have you been hiding this beautiful creature?"

"You'd be surprised." Jinx hugged her. "We've been busy being good businessmen, but it's time we take a break for ourselves. As for her, this is Onyx and she's very special to us."

"I'd guess. You don't just bring anyone here. What are we doing today, darling?" Erin asked.

A bit forward for Onyx's taste, but whatever. She'd grown accustomed to blunt people. But if nothing else, the woman could speak to her and not speak like she wasn't even there.

"Dear?" Erin stared at her. Her violet eyes shimmered and she offered a warm smile. "What are you here for? What event?"

Shit. She had been talking to Onyx. She composed herself and tried to tamp down her nerves. "I thought you were talking about me, not to me. I'm sorry. Forgive me. I truly thought you were talking to Jinx."

"It's fine, honey. If I were speaking to Jinx, then I wouldn't have expected you to come along. I'd handle this over the phone or computer and be done with it. You're here, though, and I want to make sure you're happy," Erin said. "Do you know your size?"

"I do. I'm a four. Small bust." No hips, no curves and nearly board flat. She sucked in a ragged breath. She didn't mind sharing her measurements, but not right now. In the modeling world, her size four was considered nearly full figured, compared to the size zero girls.

"Wonderful. Now, what's the event?" Erin shooed Jinx away. "We're going to find something appropriate, then she can model it for you."

"She's got the final say," Jinx said. "But sure."

She didn't bother to look over her shoulder as Erin tugged her away. "Where are we going?"

"Into the adjacent room." Erin moved a curtain aside. "In here. This is where I keep the gowns."

"How did you know I needed a gown?" She tensed. She gazed at the rack of various colors and styles of garments. Sequins, velvet, brocade, silk…she admired the cuts of the gowns and the way they shimmered. She wasn't even sure what color to choose. Normally, this was done for her—wear this for the shoot or don't wear this because you're too tall. Having to choose for herself nearly stunned her. "I'm sorry. I don't know what to say. I used to model these kinds of dresses, not wear them for myself."

"I thought you looked familiar." Erin opened a catalogue. "Look." She pointed to one of the images.

The gown was designer, in a deep black hue with strategic cutouts and requiring no undergarments. Nothing was left to the imagination—or to chance—with the dress. She turned her attention to the model, but she shouldn't have bothered. "That's me." One of her later shoots, but still an exhilarating one. "I had to tape everything down and only move when required because it stretched across my ribs."

"I'm sure it did. It's a beautiful gown, but it's cut strangely and awkward to wear. Trust designers to make something complicated," Erin said. "That's why I don't carry much couture."

"I understand that." She wanted to relax. Erin spoke her language, but she kept up her guard. "Why did you keep that image?"

"I love this catalogue. It's not current, but the dresses are much like what we've got and we can interpret them well enough to create something close."

"Wow." She exhaled, not realizing she'd held her breath.

"I know. We've got some fantastic tailors and seamstresses here." Erin stepped back and swept her gaze over Onyx. "You're definitely a four, but you're slender. Might almost be down a size."

"You think so?" She hadn't considered that. "I don't know."

"I do." She withdrew a seamstress tape from her pocket. "Let's check, after we find a gown for you. They want you to accompany them to the Delano tonight, don't they?"

"I'm not sure." They hadn't told her anything beyond a philanthropic event. "They didn't say."

"Of course they didn't." She clicked her tongue. "They're lowkey about those kinds of things, but that event is tonight, so you'll need something appropriate. What are your best colors?"

She could answer this. She straightened her posture. "I've always looked good in green—emerald green, hunter green—and red. The pastel colors don't work on me. I'm too pale for them."

"I can see that." She snapped her fingers. "I know exactly what to select for you, but if you don't like it, then we've got a couple more suggestions. Just a moment."

She waited patiently as Erin disappeared around the corner. The room had so many nooks and crannies. So many places to hide. She ran her fingers over the gowns on the racks and a lump formed in her throat. She missed dressing up in the various outfits and posing in the photos. She longed to highlight the form and cut of the different clothes. To create an effect and aura about the moment needed to wear those dresses.

Erin returned a moment later. "What do you think of this?" She arranged the dress across the arm of the sofa, spreading out the long skirt and sweeping her hand over the beading on the bodice.

"V-neck, has to be hand beaded...mermaid cut... Is that a Burreaux?" she asked. "I modeled some of those about a decade ago." Was it that long? She snorted, feeling a lot older than her twenty-eight years.

"It is." Erin beamed. "You know your designers."

"I wore her works early in her career." She touched the beading. "May I try this on?"

"I hoped you'd ask." Erin waggled her fingers. "If it fits, we're going to have you ready for tonight and we'll have you delivered to the boys. How does that sound to you?"

She didn't want to show so much enthusiasm, but damn it, she loved this. She'd be pampered and primped for them. "I can't wait. Should I tell Jinx?"

"You should, but let's see if this fits the way I think it will." Erin waggled her fingers again. "Undress."

"No one will walk in here?" What did she care? She'd been nude in front of others before. This was nothing.

"No. We're very selective about our clients and only handle one at a time. Jinx made the appointment this morning," Erin said. "Right after Zephyr did. I'm sure someone else will call my secretary wanting an appointment, but right now, you're the only one I'm serving."

"Then I can't wait to try it on." She loved beautiful clothing and this was a gorgeous gown. She shrugged out of her shirt, then toed off her shoes. Time to make herself a little bit beautiful.

Chapter Nine

Onyx luxuriated in every second of trying on gowns, having lunch brought to the store, then being prepped for the event that night. Jinx left her a note that he'd pick her back up when she was done and he'd be ready, along with Zephyr for the evening.

Her spirits soared. She loved dressing up, but having her hair done was a luxury she hadn't partaken of in a long time. She'd started cutting her own hair and worried the stylist would make a comment about the ragged job. Her fears had been for nothing. The stylist worked her magic, clipping and adjusting her hair, then styling it before spinning her around to admire her work.

Onyx loved the sleek look and soft curl.

She sat for the makeup artist and the memories of sitting for other artists came to mind. She'd been the model who could sit still while being primped. It was almost a meditation for her. She could let her mind wander and her body relax. The tension within her evaporated.

"You've done this before?" the makeup artist asked. "You're good. No wiggles or flinches."

"I'm used to it." She wanted to talk about her past, but she kept her mouth shut. Why rehash what had happened when she couldn't change or relive it?

"You've been in the chair before? Are you an actress?" the woman asked.

"No." She wasn't that good. "Just a model in my younger days."

"Younger days!" The woman snorted and stopped applying the liner for a moment. "You're not that old. What? Twenty-four?"

"Twenty-eight."

"Close enough. You're not old. I could be your mother, you know." She finished applying the makeup. "Okay, my darling. You're golden and you've got the hair. Better get yourself dressed and I'll work on your body makeup if you need it."

She'd forgotten having to do that. "Sure." She left the makeup chair and headed across the plush room to the changing space. The smaller room was like a walk-in closet. Shoes, jewelry and undergarments. She selected a pair of panties, then debated stockings.

Erin joined her in the room. "This dress won't require pantyhose. It'll get in the way of the cut. I'd stick with the panties and keep the lines clean," she said. "Let's get you into the gown. Do you wear your shoes first or wait until the last minute?"

"I always put them on first, so the hem could be adjusted one last time." She blushed from her hairline to her chest. Her skin heated. "Sorry."

"Don't have to apologize. You've been in this life and have more experience than I do, and I appreciate it. You're helping me to figure out my job, as well." Erin smiled, then trailed her fingertips over the various shoes. "You're an eight? Or nine? Closed toe or sandal?"

"Nine and a half, and pumps. I don't like my feet." She swore she blushed again. "I'm a model and supposed to love every inch of me."

"One doesn't equate the other. You're a model, so you know how to use what you've got, but you don't have to love it. I don't love every inch of me, as you say. I have huge hands."

"No, you don't." She hadn't bothered to look at them, but she knew better.

"I want to fix everyone, too." Erin selected a pair of shoes from the racks. "Here you go."

She donned the shoes, happy Erin had selected them a half a size bigger than she wore. The larger size helped for when the person wore the shoes for a while and their feet swelled a little from being on them. She straightened her spine and moved her hair from her face, then carefully stepped into the gown, paying attention not to tread on the hem. She slid the silky garment up her body, then threaded her arms through the thin straps. As she adjusted the dress on her frame, she sucked in a quick breath as Erin zipped her in. She wasn't ready to look at herself just yet.

"Nervous?" Erin asked.

"Petrified." She met Erin's gaze. "I haven't had this kind of lavish treatment in so long. I was used to it from modeling, but I haven't lived that life in forever."

"You're entitled."

"Maybe, but I don't feel entitled." She felt unworthy.

"No, I mean, you're permitted to want to be cherished."

"Why are you so sure? I don't even have a concept of how much Jinx and Zephyr spent on this outing. It has to be a lot." And she worried she'd never be able to pay them back.

"The cost isn't important, to be honest. It's part of being on the arm of the two wealthiest men in the county. They have to look the role of expensive men about town and you've got to be equally fantastic to be beside them. You already know how to do that, now it's just a matter of putting it all together. You're doing it."

"I'm trying." She hated sounding so concerned.

"You're succeeding." Erin turned her around to face the mirror. "See? You're a vision and they'll have one hell of a hard time not paying you full attention. They'll be all over you and might not even last the night. That's a good thing."

It was. She drank in the image of herself. The gown clung to her like a second skin. The fabric accentuated her slight curves and brought out the color in her eyes. The makeup artist had worked magic, along with the fantastic haircut...she stole her own breath. "Wow."

"I know, right?" Erin winked as she met her gaze in the reflection. "I knew that dress was you."

"It doesn't leave much room for me to not be me." She smoothed her hands over her hips. "I just need a clutch and wrap, then I'll be ready. Am I too early?"

"Oh, honey, it's past six. Almost seven." Erin produced a clutch, then a simple crocheted wrap. "This will finish the look."

"Thanks." She slid the soft garment around her shoulders, then held onto the purse. She didn't have anything to put in the clutch at the moment, but she'd figure something out. "How much do I owe you?"

"Me? Nothing. Honey, I want to be your personal stylist from now on. You're easy to style and even easier to work with. You're the kind of client I dream of." Erin opened the door. "But right now, your beaus are waiting. They're here in the foyer."

"They're here?" Her breath quickened and she whimpered. She might not be on display in cuffs or a bandage outfit at the club. Hell, she was more covered than the first night they'd met, but she swore she was completely bare. She managed to put one foot in front of the other and walked out to the foyer, following Erin. When she rounded the doorway into the outer room, Jinx and Zephyr turned. They both wore tuxedos and looked like visions.

Who were the true lucky ones? Them or her? She was going to be on the arms of two of the hottest bachelors in the county. They'd have a pretty girl with them.

She wanted to speak, but her voice was gone. She pressed her lips together. *Just breathe.*

"Hello." Jinx offered his arm first. "My God, you're beautiful."

"Thank you," she managed. She loosened her grasp on the wrap and turned. "Erin did a great job."

"She sure did." Zephyr swept her into his arms. "I don't know if we'll make it to the dinner."

"You will," Erin said. "You're receiving the award for philanthropy tonight."

"Unfortunately, she's correct." Jinx patted Onyx's ass. "But that doesn't mean we can't enjoy ourselves on the way."

"We can." She wasn't ashamed to say such things. These two men did care about her. Maybe they might even love her. She'd make them happy.

Zephyr held onto her, but spoke to Erin. "Thank you, as always, for your work. We knew we were smart to leave her in your deft hands."

"I expect it'll be a wonderful night," Erin said. "Treat her right."

"We will." Jinx let go long enough to kiss Erin on the cheek, then joined Zephyr as they left the shop.

Onyx didn't bother to argue as she allowed them to escort her to the car. She stopped short. "You seriously had a limo brought in?"

"We do have to keep up appearances," Zephyr said. "And you're stunning, so you fit right in."

"I'm good arm candy?" She laughed as they opened the door for her.

"You're not just another sweet smile." Zephyr allowed her into the car first, then joined on her right.

Jinx hurried in behind them and sat on her left as the driver closed the door. He patted her thigh. "Won't be able to keep my hands off you."

"I second that." Zephyr massaged her other thigh. "Although I should probably stop doing this so we don't muss your dress."

She shrugged. "It won't hurt it to wrinkle it a little." She didn't care what they did as long as she could be with them. Crinkles in her dress could be smoothed. Sure, she excelled at being put together, but even the most polished person wasn't perfect.

"You're so cavalier." Jinx laced her fingers with his. "We're the luckiest men in the building."

"In the world." Zephyr stretched his legs. "I don't mind giving the money to this stuff, but I hate getting awards. Feels so fake."

"It can be," she said. "When I was starting out modeling, after I had to reignite my career, I was given the chance to accept an award on behalf of a local actress. She'd won an award, but broken her foot right before the ceremony. I guess she didn't want anyone to see her in a cast and gown, so they wanted someone to accept it. She did a video link to accept it, but I walked onto the stage. It was kind of cool to be her for a second, but also so fake. Everyone knew it wasn't her, but I was the one on stage."

"I'd like a placeholder," Jinx muttered. "Then we could be home in bed."

"You're too cranky," Zephyr said. "I know how we can make this much more exciting."

"Oh?" She tipped her head. "And that's how?"

"This." He held up a bullet vibrator. "You know what to do with this."

She did. She'd need a little help adjusting her dress to insert the toy, but she couldn't wait. He held the vibrator in one and his phone in the other.

"I'm sending the app to Jinx, so we both have control over it." Zephyr crooked his brow. "You know what to do."

"Don't you dare lose it." Jinx smoothed her dress up, exposing her thighs.

"I won't." She stopped his hands. "Just a minute." She moved the hook and zipper along the slit to the dress.

"So that's how you can use the ladies' room in that gown." Zephyr slid his gaze over her legs. "Damn."

She scooted in her seat. "Do you want to do the honors?"

Zephyr tugged her panties aside enough to finger her cunt. He toyed with her pussy lips. "You're wet."

Hell yes, she was. She shivered and bit back a groan. She met his gaze. "I want to please you, Sir."

"Do you?" He slid his finger into her pussy. "So hot and tight." He pumped his digit, drawing a groan from deep in her chest.

She grasped Jinx's hand. "Fuck."

"Feels good?" Jinx murmured. He eased his arm around her shoulders. He cupped her breast, caressing her. Her nipple beaded. She dug her heels into the carpet, trying to steady herself.

"There we go." Zephyr withdrew his finger, then inserted the toy. "Don't you dare lose that."

"I won't." She ground her teeth together to fight off the waves of pleasure flowing through her body. She could have all the excitement she could handle, as long as she kept her composure.

With Zephyr's help, she managed to put the zipper back into place and hook the closure after smoothing her dress down. He hadn't even turned the toy on, but she already had shivers. She bit back another groan.

"Good girl." Zephyr kissed her cheek. "The struggle won't be yours alone. Not sure how I'll keep the erection at bay, knowing I can bring you pleasure."

At least he'd suffer the exquisite frustration, too.

Jinx pinched her nipple through the bodice of her dress. "Ever consider piercing them?"

"My nipples?" She leaned into him. "I did, but it wasn't appreciated if you're a model. We're supposed to remain blemish free, if at all possible." He could touch and pinch whatever part of her he wanted. She loved the delicious pain. It spurred her on. It also made thinking almost impossible. She wasn't sure how she was forming coherent sentences and she'd be in trouble during dinner if they turned on the toy.

"I suppose you're right." Jinx pinched once more, then rubbed her bare arm. "It'd be hot on you, but if you want to work, then you have to do what you have to do."

Oddly put, but he was right.

The car stopped and she leaned into her seat. "We're here?"

"We are." Zephyr tucked his phone into his pocket. "Are you ready?" He offered his arm.

"I am." For anything. She eased the wrap around her upper body, then her arm around his as he helped her from the car. She walked with him into the building. She'd done a few building openings and gala events, so the procedure didn't bother her. The flashes from the cameras and the shouting were part of the process.

"You're handling this like a champ." Jinx took his place beside her, pinning her between them. "Like you've done this before."

"I have." She stole a glance at him and admired the striking man. He and Zephyr were indeed gorgeous men, but they were not only handsome on the outside, but glowing from the inside. They were the kinds of men that were the stuff of dreams.

And she was between them.

She smiled for the cameras and waited for each time she was asked to pose. She'd done things like this before, but never with a vibrator in her pussy. A shiver rocked through her. God, keeping a straight face tonight would be impossible, and they hadn't even turned the toy on.

"Ready?" Zephyr led the way into the building. He stopped to shake hands with various people and nodded to both Jinx and Onyx. "I arrived with my partners," he said to whomever seemed to listen.

At the word partners, her spirits perked. She glanced at Jinx, who beamed.

"Oh?" A woman stepped up to them and extended her hand. "Hello, again."

"Hello, Jeannie."

"So you're here with your...business partners?" Jeannie asked. "You and Mr. Collins are related, yes?"

"No and you know that." Zephyr shook his head. "Best friends, and Ms. Power is our third." He crooked his brow, then stepped away.

Onyx followed him and forced her gaze straight ahead. She refused to embarrass Jeannie more.

"Wow," Jinx said as they reached the table. "You really slayed her. I mean, savage. Jeannie isn't that bad."

"You were a bit cruel," Onyx added. "I mean, you could've been more kind."

"I've known Jeannie for years." Zephyr held the back of the chair for Onyx. "She wasn't trying to be kind, as you put it. We do work for her as landscapers, but she can be scathing when provoked."

"That's terrible." Onyx hesitated before sitting. "Was she trying to be snarky?" She didn't know the woman, but sort of pitied her. Some people were terrible at small talk and others were clueless. Sometimes, unintentionally clueless.

"She was." Jinx sat on her left side. "Jeannie made a play for Zeph a few years ago. She knows he and I aren't related. She also knew others were listening, so if it brought Zeph down a peg, then great."

"That's rotten." She tensed as one of them turned on the vibrator. *Holy fucking hell.* She pressed her toes together in her shoes and tensed from the waist down. Every cell in her body vibrated. She kept her hands on her lap to hide the ripples of pleasure going through her being.

"Like that?" Zephyr asked. He sat on her right and palmed her thigh. "I saw your eyes light up."

"I felt the groan you're trying to hide." Jinx slid his arm across the back of her chair. "Feels good, doesn't it?"

She nodded, for fear she'd squeal if she tried to speak.

"I believe so." Zephyr snorted and picked up his water glass. "Going to be a wonderful night."

She agreed fully. Onyx crossed her ankles. She kept her poise, but she wasn't sure how. Within a few moments, a server filled the wineglasses, then adjusted the candles on the table. An announcer spoke, but Onyx only heard about half of what was said. Every time she thought she'd adjusted to the feel of the vibrations, either Jinx or Zephyr changed the speed or frequency. She'd never be able to hold herself together.

Onyx reached for the wineglass and prayed her hands wouldn't shake. She sipped the dry red wine and closed her eyes for a moment.

Jinx brushed a stray lock of hair from her cheek. "Feels good?" he murmured. "Want to have my cock buried so deep inside you? My hands on your ass, spanking you?"

She opened her eyes and carefully put the glass down. "I do." She stole a glance at him. "I so want that."

"You'll get it." Jinx caressed her shoulder.

The combination of his fingers on her skin and the toy in her pussy was nearly her undoing. She bit back a gasp. She couldn't wait to get home.

The announcer spoke again and plates were brought to the tables. For the first time since Jinx and Zephyr turned on the vibrator, they turned it off. She exhaled and finally relaxed her hands.

"Eat, sweetheart. You've made me happy." Jinx kissed her cheek. "Very much."

"Very much so." Zephyr winked. "Enjoy your dinner. We've got the award soon, then we can go home."

She couldn't wait.

Chapter Ten

Zephyr practically ran to the car after the banquet finished. He didn't want to pose for photos or attract more attention. Hell, he hated attention like that and it'd been most of the reason he and Jinx had been given the award. They'd donated a large sum of money and kept quiet about it.

Now the media in the area wanted to keep talking about what they'd done.

He rushed to the car and opened the door for Onyx. The toy play made being at the banquet fun, yet excruciating because he wanted to sneak off to the bathroom or one of the side rooms to make love to her.

"Excuse me."

He glanced back at Jeannie. "Do you need something?"

She grasped his arm, drawing him away from the car. "A moment of your time."

He bit back a sigh. "Sure." She drove him crazy, but he'd speak to her. "What's on your mind?"

"You're seeing someone," Jeannie said. "She's cute."

"We are and she is." He hated wasting time.

"A bit young, isn't she?"

"She's only four years younger than you." Onyx was young, but not by that much.

"I see." Jeannie offered a stony gaze. "You said you'd call."

"I said we would see each other." He'd never made her promises and didn't want to waste her time, either. He swept his gaze over her. Once, he'd thought he might be attracted to her as a lover. He'd considered holding her, kissing her…being with her. But the more he looked at her, the more he considered the glare in her eyes and the venom in her voice, the more he appreciated his decision to keep their relationship businesslike.

"I thought we had something," she said, her voice soft. "We got along."

"We did get along, but we weren't going to work. You want different things than I do." He should be in the car with Jinx and Onyx. He'd rather be spending time with them.

"I could want what you do."

"You could, but is that being true to who you are?" He'd been through this with her. "You need to do what's best for you, not what you think I want." Why did people think they had to change for each other? To be with someone should mean to be yourself and the best version of yourself, not to fit into the mold they'd set for you.

She groaned. "Why are you being so difficult?"

"What do you mean? I'm trying to help and save you time. Do you really want to waste months or years on someone who can't be who you need? No. You should be chasing a man who can keep up with you. A man who sees your bold nature and loves it. A man who isn't afraid of your sharp tongue. That's not me. I'm not afraid of you, but I'm not good for you, either," he said. "We're meant to be partners in business, not love."

"You're trying to save me time?" She clicked her tongue. "That's a riot and a lie."

"I'm attempting to be kind, but you're trying my patience. I could get short with you," he said, his voice even. "I'm saving you the effort of trying to land someone who isn't interested. I want a woman who is herself—not trying to be what I want. It's difficult because we all try to belong, but we deserve to be happy and I won't make you happy."

"You could if you tried."

"Nah." He wasn't that kind of man. "I only try when I want to and I have other things I want to do."

"Like her."

"Crass." Why did she have to be so cruel?

"What else should I call her? She's obviously a gold-digger."

"Stop. This isn't like you." Plus, he was wasting so much time. He sighed. "Look, I'm not interested and I'm sorry. You're a nice woman who will make another man happy, so try to find him—he's not me."

"So you and your cousin have moved on?"

His irritation grew. "You made a point of griping about that earlier. He's my friend and partner, but we're not related. I'll kindly ask you to stop saying anything else." She'd been warned. "I'm late."

"For what?"

"Leaving." He sidestepped her. He'd been nice for long enough. "I need to go."

"You need to be real." She invaded his path again. "She's young, doesn't appear very bright and is very much more interested in Jinx. I can see it in her eyes. She'll be with the both of you, but she'd like money and she'd rather have him."

The barb cut deep. He hated the wedge being driven between the three of them, even if the insult wasn't true. Besides, if Jeannie had seen a particular look in Onyx's eyes, it was the glazed expression due to the vibrator.

"So stop trying to shoehorn her and everyone else into being with both of you. It won't work. You need a woman and he needs another. Let him have her and I'll make you happy. I can do it." She grasped his lapels. "Please."

"You should never have to throw yourself at a man." He backed away from her. "You're better than that."

"What?"

"You're better than having to beg and plead with anyone. You run your own business—a successful one—and you're respected by your peers. You need a partner, sure. No one wants to be alone, which I get, but you should never settle for someone because you're lonely. You accept only the best from your employees and demand the best for your customers. Why should you lower yourself for a romance?"

She opened her mouth, but no sound came out. A moment of fear shimmered in her eyes.

"You know I'm right," he replied.

She shrugged, trying to regain her composure, no doubt. She let go of his jacket. "Well."

"Well?" That made little sense. "Well what?"

"You enjoy your friend and friend. When it falls apart with her, don't try to find me."

He hadn't planned on it—not for romance. For business, sure. "My men will be there on Monday to take care of the landscaping." He'd never cut those ties.

"No you won't. I'll hire someone else. Your services are no longer needed." She turned on her heel and strode away.

"Well...shit." He wasn't expecting to be dismissed. Hell, she confused him with her reply. He'd thought they had a decent working relationship. Sure, it wasn't going to be romantic, but...fuck.

As long as Jeannie didn't try to smear him and use retribution to get back at him for this perceived slight, he'd be fine, but he'd have to be on guard. Word of mouth still held weight for his business and among his peers. He wanted to keep his business strong and his working relationships stronger.

Fuck.

He'd have to talk to Jinx about this, though. Sooner than later.

He opened the car door, but his thoughts were a mess. He'd thought he'd been kind in his response to Jeannie. He'd had a wonderful time with Onyx, teasing her and basking in the glory of attending the ceremony with two of the best people in the world. Yet, his heart ached. He worried he'd made a mistake in his wording with Jeannie.

Christ, he needed a break.

A trip would be good.

After the publicity work was finished. The sooner he got Onyx working, the more she'd feel independent and her true spirit would shine.

He settled on the seat in the back of the car. "Fuck me."

"You took your sweet time," Jinx said. "Got lost?"

"I'd fuck you," Onyx murmured. "And him."

Zephyr ensured he hadn't turned the vibrator on by accident and closed the app. "Would you believe Jeannie stopped me?"

"Again?" Jinx rolled his eyes. "Figures. I thought I saw her out there."

"Jeannie?" Onyx asked. "It's not my business. Sorry."

"She's the woman who stopped us before we went in for dinner. She wanted to be my girlfriend and never was — sort of like the others who keep trying to push in, only to be the wrong fit." Zephyr groaned. "People will do anything to get ahead on the back of someone else."

"What did she want now?" Jinx asked.

"Long story short, I turned her down and she fired our contractor and threw some money at us to complete the contract. We no longer handle the landscaping at her firm."

"So tit for tat," Jinx snapped. "I should've guessed."

"She didn't like being scorned?" Onyx asked. "So she fired you?"

"In a word, yes." He shifted in his seat. "She does that." And in a few months, she'd probably change her mind and rehire them.

"I guess it's her loss." Onyx grasped his hand. "I'm sure you did the right thing."

"I did, but she's got a nasty revenge streak. She doesn't like being turned down or disrespected — even if it's only in her mind." He respected Jeannie's determination and tenacity, but if those were born out of vitriol, not competition, his respect dwindled. "She's angry I won't be with her and I'm worried she'll take it out on our business."

"That's silly," Onyx replied. "She didn't get her way. So what? Grow up and move forward."

"Nacin didn't," he said without thinking. "Shit. I mean…" He'd fucked up.

"Sorry." She withdrew into herself.

"No," Jinx replied. "What Zeph is poorly trying to say is that she didn't get what she wanted, much like Nacin, and she'll be cruel to make up for that slight — even if it's not true. She'll want to ruin us for spite."

"Sure," Onyx muttered. "I suppose you're right, but you don't have to be so cruel." She remained tucked into herself.

"I wasn't…" He'd realized his mistake as soon as he'd spoken, but there was little way to fix this. He'd been terrible to her, when he'd actually meant his vitriol for Jeannie and the others who'd irked him. "I'm sorry."

"I know you are." She kept her gaze low. "It's fine."

It wasn't fine at all. His phone buzzed, interrupting his thoughts. Probably the crew alerting him to the job change. He checked the notification — an alert from Keifer.

Christ, this wasn't what he wanted.

He swiped to retrieve the message.

Check hasn't arrived and transfer didn't go through. Bounced? Insufficient funds? Or a change of heart?

A dull ache formed behind his eyes. Keifer had some nerve to annoy him to such an extreme degree.

"What?" Jinx leaned forward. "More shit hitting the fan?"

"Sort of." He'd make a call when they arrived at the house. "Nothing major." He put the phone away. There was too much anger in the world and he wasn't about to let it ruin his night even further. He'd unintentionally hurt Onyx because of his frustration. Not cool. Not kind. What a dick.

"Almost to the house," Jinx said. "We can forget the night and have fun."

"Yeah." Onyx sighed. "I suppose so."

He had so much damage control and groveling to do. The car stopped and Onyx scrambled out first. His heart hammered. He doubted she'd be so rash as to leave, but he needed to get in front of the rest of the shit happening. "Sweetheart?" He rushed after her. "Slow down." How in the hell was she so fast in those high heels?

"I'll be fine." She didn't look back.

"I know you will." He touched her hand. "Stop, please?"

She halted, but didn't turn around. "Yes?"

"I get you're upset and I know I'm the cause. I deserve every bit of your anger. I'm not always nice, but I should be kind to you and I wasn't. My being stressed isn't a good enough reason and you shouldn't accept it. I want to make this up to you and want you to give me another chance." He had a few ideas how this might happen.

"Sir."

"Please?"

She finally turned. "Okay."

"I plan to delight in you and spoil you. You, Jinx and I will love every second."

Her eyes glittered. "I'm still irritated with you, but yes, Sir."

"I know you are and I'll make it up to you after I straighten this out. Why don't you go to our room and wait on the bed? Sit on the edge of the bed, but don't get undressed. I want to unwrap you like the gift you are. Do you wish to play?"

"A scene?"

"Yes." *Without a doubt.*

"I do, Sir. My safe word is pumpkin and I don't wish to use it."

"Very well." He swatted her on the rump. "Jinx and I will be just a moment."

"Yes, Sir." She darted forward and kissed him on the cheek before rushing off.

He grinned as she disappeared down the hallway. She deserved the moon and stars. She certainly should have someone better than a damaged man like him.

Jinx strode up to him. "I tried to give you a moment. Is everything okay?"

"Yes and no." He scrubbed the back of his hand across his forehead. "Besides the issue of Jeannie — which time will tell — Keifer texted. He's going to be a pain in our collective ass."

"Oh? Already?" Jinx shook his head. "I knew he'd get anxious. Lemme guess. He thinks he didn't get the money and he's being a dick?"

"Pretty much." He stared at his best friend. "You know something I don't?"

"Yeah, I sent a fake transfer. It should've looked real, but it wasn't. Should've been followed by a bad check. If he read it, which I doubt he did, it's made out to Gotufuker. I'm serious." Jinx bobbed his brows. "I wanted him to crawl and squirm."

"He slithered."

"I'm sure."

"He's pissed the check didn't clear and that the transfer didn't go through. He thinks we might have changed our minds," Zephyr said. "I don't know if he read it, but he didn't get his money and he's being difficult."

"Good. Then I got under his skin."

"You did," Zephyr said. "He's determined to make life miserable for us until we pay him."

"For long after, too."

"I'd assume so."

"I want a pound of flesh from him before he gets any cash," Jinx replied. He's a rat and needs to pay. I'm not letting him off easy."

"Who says we are?" Zephyr leaned on the table in the foyer. "What if we talk to Xavier Green? If he really owns the club, then he should want to know the shit Keifer is pulling. I doubt he'll like it because it's bad for his business."

"We could ruin Keifer, yes." Jinx nodded and stuffed his hands into his pockets. "I'm in. That club needs better than Keifer and honestly, it's not a bad place, but he'll run it into the ground."

"When the truth comes out, yes." The more he thought about his idea to contact Xavier, the more he liked it.

"I don't want to give Keifer a cent," Jinx said. "We go to Xavier and see what he wants. He might not realize what Keifer's doing."

"He might not." He doubted it completely.

"I did some research this afternoon while I was waiting on her to try on clothes," Jinx said. "On Keifer. He's connected to Nacin. Not just friends or business acquaintances. They're closer."

His blood chilled. "Fuck."

"Uh-huh." Jinx glanced over his shoulder. "That's why she's in debt so deeply. They worked out a deal.

Keifer keeps her out of sight and Nacin exacts his revenge. She'll never get out of debt and she's not working, so she won't pay it off. Plus, she's not out in public, which means they control the narrative."

"Meaning they can smear her reputation and make money off her back? That's disgusting."

"It's vile." Jinx shrugged. "It's their only play because Keifer is drowning in debt and Nacin has most likely assaulted other women, but no one has been bold enough, except for her, to stand up to him. Nacin can't stand being turned down or challenged and Keifer's in the hole. If they control her, then no one knows the truth."

"Except us." The fuckers. He gritted his teeth. "And we champion her."

"She thinks she's not strong enough to handle this, but what she doesn't understand is that she's powerful. She managed to force them both to their knees and this is their only way to handle it. It's fucked up, yet, she got their attention. She also got ours and didn't back down."

"And now they think they're going to take us out in the process." He nodded once. "I'm contacting Xavier. This is shit."

"Tomorrow." Jinx rapped his knuckles on the doorway. "We need to get back to her and spend all evening reassuring her that things will be okay."

"Should tell her the truth, too." But he needed to handle this first. "Go be with her for now. She's waited for long enough and deserves attention, but I need to do something."

Jinx hesitated. "You're going to find him tonight, aren't you?"

"Bingo. This has to end. She won't be able to focus until this charade is over and we have so much we can do. She's got an entire career ahead of her and should be able to enjoy it."

"They don't realize who they've pissed off, do they?" Jinx asked.

"No, but did you think they would?" He shrugged. "I'll be back." He turned on his heel, then strode to the garage. He'd use one of their drivers for this mission so he had a way home and a witness, too.

Calvin, the driver they'd used for the banquet, exited the sedan before closing the door gently. "Were there any issues tonight?"

"No. You were fine." He clapped Calvin on the shoulder. "I need a favor. I need to go to Sixxes. Care to take me?"

"You're going to cause trouble, aren't you?" Calvin laughed and shook his head. "Need a witness?"

"I might." His driver knew them too well.

"Then by all means. Let's go." Calvin opened the door to the sports car and gestured to the passenger seat. "You know I love going on these adventures."

He rounded the trunk and joined him in the vehicle. "What do you think of Onyx?"

"To be honest, she's the best one you've brought home. She seems sweet and authentic. A couple of the others weren't so much, and it's refreshing to have someone here who treats us like we're not just the help," Calvin said. "She ran into Sarah when Sarah was changing the sheets and she offered to give her a hand. None of the others would've done that."

"True." He marveled at Onyx's ability to be relatable.

"She just seems real and it's nice. She also doesn't seem to want your money, which is also refreshing." Calvin left the property. "You both really like her?"

"We do." He'd fallen hard for her and wasn't ready to give her up. Hell, he wanted to champion her like he'd never done before.

"Good. Keep her around. She's humble." Calvin drove across town and within half an hour, parked in the garage at Sixxes. "You're going to be okay?"

"I will." He pulled the handgun from the glove box and tucked it in his waistband. For being the head of a company, he wasn't above bringing a piece when needed. He concealed the weapon and patted his breast pocket to ensure he'd brought his wallet, then left the car. "I'll be right back."

"I'll be here and ready to leave on your signal and watching for whatever happens out here." Calvin rolled the window up, but cut the engine.

He adjusted his jacket cuffs, then strode into the club. Once he reached the desk, he winked at the woman behind the counter. "I need to speak to Danger."

"Oh." She swiped the screen on her tablet. "Um…he's not here tonight."

"I know he's here." He'd spied Danger's name on the list. "Now, do you want to waste my time? Or work with me?"

She blushed. "I'm supposed to make you wait until Mr. Jones arrives. He doesn't want you speaking to Danger." Her blush ran from her hairline to her chest. "My job isn't worth the shit he's going to give me."

"No, it's not." He nodded twice. "Where is Danger? Keifer can find me when he's finished doing whatever he's doing."

"Danger is in the main room. He's watching tonight, not playing. Silver vest, black pants and he's tipped his hair in silver glitter." She turned the tablet over. "I don't suppose you have a spot for a secretary for one of your contractors? I'm so going to get fired for this."

"I'll see what I can do. Talk to HR on Monday." He rapped his knuckles on the counter, then strode right into the playroom. He'd find Danger if it was the last thing he did.

Chapter Eleven

Zephyr located Xavier right away. How could he miss the silver glitter and sequins? He snorted. The look wasn't his idea of sexy, but it worked for Xavier. He marched into the playroom, passing a few of the subs he recognized, but not seeing Keifer. *Interesting.*

He kept going, but a blonde sub stepped into his path.

He groaned. What was it with people getting in his way? He crooked his brow, but said nothing.

She grinned. "Hi. Funny seeing you here. Are you alone?"

"A bit forward for a house sub." He narrowed his eyes. "Excuse me."

"I heard you're looking for a new sub. I want to volunteer to be yours." She reached for him. "Please?"

"Wow." He shook his head. "No, thank you. I'm fine." He turned his attention to Xavier. He kept moving and didn't look back at her. As he stopped next to the sofa where Xavier sat, he nodded once.

Xavier noticed him right away and straightened his shoulders. "Sir."

"Good boy." He snapped his fingers. "I have a proposition for you. Do you want to join me?"

"I do, Sir. Thank you, Sir." Xavier stood, then bowed his head and fell in step just behind Zephyr.

Instead of stopping in one of the playrooms, he directed Xavier to the changing area. "I want you to come with me."

"Sir?" Xavier stopped just inside the changing room. "Where are we going?"

"For a drive." He held out his hand. "Do you want to go with me, Danger?"

"I do. Thank you, Sir." He grasped Zephyr's hand and followed him out of the building to the car.

Zephyr allowed Xavier into the backseat first, then joined him. Once the door closed, the car moved.

"I bet you're wondering what brought me out tonight," Zephyr said. "Or why I'd ask you to join me."

"It occurred to me." Xavier folded his arms. "You're not here for a scene. I know the girl you've chosen. She's pretty and sweet…she also happens to belong to Keifer."

"I see." He had to measure his words carefully. "I didn't know you knew that."

"I know a lot more than everyone thinks." Xavier sighed and shifted from a sweet-natured sub to a businessman in seconds. "He believes I'm not paying attention. I know what he's doing."

"Do you?" He toyed with the armrest. "Did you know he's using her?"

"I had the feeling he was." Xavier shook his head. "How much does he have on her? A million? More?"

"You knew about that?" He'd hoped so.

"Yeah. I've been looking at the books and registrations. She's not the only woman into him for money, but she's the one who seems to be in the deepest and with the silliest reasons," Xavier said. "She's been on the schedule and working, but she's not on the payroll. When I questioned Keifer, he claimed she wanted to be paid under the table. I don't play that way. If you're working for the club, then you're doing it legitimately."

"I agree," he replied. "It's the smartest way to handle business."

"Among other things, but yes." Xavier relaxed. "You picked up on me being there. How'd you know it was me?"

"You stand out, while not standing out at all."

Xavier chuckled. "I guess so. I never considered anyone would actually hunt for me. I've been hiding in plain sight for so long."

"You have." He stopped playing with the armrest. "She's into him for a lot of money and my research says it's not on the books because that's his way of keeping her subservient to him."

"He's working with Nacin, isn't he?" Xavier groaned. "Fucker. I knew he was pulling something shady."

"You figured it out?" He wished he'd have known that sooner.

"I did, but recently. I don't like to pay much attention to the club. It's supposed to be a place for me to have fun and let go. That's why I allowed Keifer to run it, but I see that was a mistake. He's not the trustworthy man I used to know."

"He's not." He tipped his head. "You were friends with him before?"

"We grew up together. Seems like a million years ago now. We were kids in Illinois. He was a year behind me, but it was like having a brother. We talked about everything and when I started making money, he followed along. When he got a few breaks, he shared his good fortune. Our plan was good until I started making stupid money and he wasn't. I couldn't drag him along that far. He wanted me to do it for him. Yeah, no. He'd started mixing with people I didn't know and wasn't fond of, but that had to be his path. I had to go on mine. The way we crossed again was at the club. I needed someone I thought I could trust and he seemed like he could be trusted. I was wrong."

"We've all been wrong about people that we cared about. It's life." He understood that well. "Don't beat yourself up over that."

"I don't, but I'm angry with him. He got involved with Nacin and I knew there was something more to the friendship. Money seemed more prevalent and there have been women working the club that aren't the usual girls. Her, for example. She might have been there to play, not work, if it hadn't been for him."

"I know."

"He let it slip tonight that he's coming into a big score. So I did some research. I found the messages on the computer—he never bothered to hide them," Xavier said. "And he named her."

"He didn't expect you to go looking."

"He didn't."

"He not only named her, but he named what he was going to do with her. He was going to extort you both for money and hold her for ransom." Xavier shook his head. "I knew she was with you, which is why I wasn't too worried. If I'd have guessed she'd come in, then I'd have acted differently."

"I understand." He gritted his teeth. "Doesn't make me less angry." He knew to his core he'd be extorted because of this situation.

"I expected you to be pissed. Hell, I'd have been shocked if you weren't. She's a good girl and he's using her. I don't claim to know what possessed him to do it, other than money, and I don't understand at all why she felt she had to defer to him. He didn't think I'd be upset," Xavier said. "That's why I went with you. We weren't going to be able to talk at the club because he's got ears everywhere. He's just not smart enough to realize someone else might be watching him, too."

He nodded. He'd had enough of this charade with Keifer. "So what do you want to do? We've decided we're keeping Onyx."

"She's okay with being kept?"

"She is." She seemed to be. For a man with loads of confidence, he doubted his decision.

"Then do your damn level best to keep her safe. Don't let her out of your sight without being fucking creepy. I'm serious. Don't you dare let her come back here."

"Never said I would, but I'd like to make a plan about the fucker. I know what I want to do, but I need you on my side." He leveled his gaze at Xavier. "I get it that you want to play and fly under the radar. Don't blame you for that. But we need to stop him."

"What's your suggestion? I'm listening."

"I've tried to do a fake transfer, but he seems to have noticed. He's angry the money isn't coming through," he said. "I don't doubt the club needs cash."

"It's not going under, but we can always use upgrades."

"So then I present him with a check, but the money actually goes to the club in a way he can't touch it, but the club benefits. He thinks he's getting a windfall, but it's not going to him at all." He'd write a dummy check to Keifer and a legitimate one to the club through Xavier.

"Go through the company," Xavier said. "It's there just as a front for the club. People are happier to give money to the club when their statement doesn't mention a sex club. I know the cash is coming and I'll make sure it's used for the right reasons. Name the room and it's going there."

"Her reputation stays out of it?"

"Of course. If I'd have known earlier what he was doing, I'd have shut it down faster. My regret is not paying attention long ago." Xavier rocked forward as the car stopped. He ruffled his hair and smeared the glitter on his cheek. "Gotta keep up the ruse we did something. Can't go back nicer than I left."

"Understood."

"Write the check to him for whatever amount you think is ridiculous and will get his attention. The donation for the club can be whatever you think is possible, but make sure you send it to the company. You should have the information."

"I do."

"Good. I've got an idea what I'll do to castrate him for his stupidity. You fuck with him and I'll do the same. He's dying to meet Ian Mulrone."

"Who's that?" He'd never heard of the man.

"The sham owner of the club. I'm the one on the other end of the paperwork, but he thinks it's the model

I hired to be the face. If he knew the truth, Keifer would lose his mind. He never has to know, but that doesn't mean I can't mess with him. He's messed with her and now you and Jinx. It's time for him to fall. Time for Nacin to finally look like the shit he is." Xavier rumpled his shirt, then winked. "We'll fix this and she'll be able to fly high again."

"She will." He shook hands with Xavier. "We'll take good care of her. Thank you." How could they not? He waited for Xavier to exit before leaning back in his seat and sighing. "Fuck."

He massaged his temples. He'd become accustomed to people trying to get money for their own purposes. Everyone wanted something for nothing and they'd work so hard to get that something. If they'd just spend the energy on doing the right thing or at least for good, they'd be unstoppable. But why do something for yourself when one could steal it instead?

He and Jinx had built themselves up. They made the business work and now they could enjoy the spoils of their efforts. He glanced at the clock and a groan rumbled in his throat. It was well past three in the morning. He'd wasted too many minutes and doubted she'd be awake. She was a great sub, but even the best subs eventually collapsed from exhaustion.

He shook his head and waited for Calvin to take him home. He'd spent far too much time away and needed to spend more with the ones he loved. Jinx was the brother he'd never had and Onyx was the third they'd been looking for. If it were up to him, they'd never let her go.

When the car pulled into the garage, he yawned. The time of night finally caught up to him and he stretched in his seat. Fuck it. They weren't going to have a scene tonight, but they could in the morning. Besides, they'd have time then to plan out the scene, plus the rest of the day…or three.

As light poured into the car when Calvin opened the door, Zephyr sighed. He left the vehicle. His legs ached, but he pressed forward. He'd been sitting for too long and needed to move. "Thanks, Cal."

"You're welcome. Get some rest. We all need it, but I'll be ready if you want me to drive you around tomorrow." Calvin closed the car door. He wiped the handle, making the chrome shine before running the cloth over the fender.

"Take the day off. We're staying in and you should see your wife." He and Jinx worked Calvin too hard.

"Will do." Calvin laughed before leaving him in the garage.

Zephyr made his way into the house and kicked off his shoes in the side room. Normally, he didn't leave his belongings out, but he'd worry about them in the morning. He trudged through the home to the bedroom. When he turned the corner and stepped into the dimly lit space, he spied Onyx and Jinx on the bed. She'd changed out of her dress and into a button down — probably one of Jinx's — and lay on her side. Jinx, his shirt off, but pants still on, snuggled up behind her. Both were fast asleep.

The image of them together pleased him, yet brought out a tiny streak of jealousy. He wanted to be tangled up with them. He shrugged out of his jacket, then shirt before tugging off his socks. He switched off the light. When he crawled onto the bed, neither Jinx or Onyx moved. He stretched out against Onyx and dragged a blanket over the three of them. Sleep overtook him. He'd worry about the shit with Keifer, the check for Xavier, and getting her first shoot booked tomorrow.

* * * *

When he opened his eyes, he breathed in the scent of Onyx's hair. The floral perfume relaxed him. He tightened his grasp on her waist, tucking her tighter to his midsection.

She stretched, grinding into him. "You've had a hold of me all night."

"Since I got back." He hated himself for taking so much time away from them.

"You did," she whispered. She turned slightly to look into his eyes. "What took so long?"

He hesitated a moment as Jinx snored, then rolled onto his other side with his back to them.

He might as well be honest with her. "I found out what's going on. I'll explain further when Jinx wakes, but I know what Keifer is doing and I put a stop to it."

"Oh?" Jinx stirred. He rolled back to face them and scrubbed his hand across his forehead. "You got it all straight?"

"Long story short. Keifer's in debt up to his eyeballs and not just financially. He's into Nacin for money, into the club, into Xavier…it's a mess. Nacin doesn't want you out in public because you're the key to his downfall. If you push your complaint against him and anything comes out, he can't argue it because he's guilty as sin. So Keifer, to help pay off his debts, has you working at the club, has you out of sight, so you're not spotlighting Nacin's behavior and they win. Xavier figured it out and so have we. Xavier's working with us to stop it. You live your life, model, speak your truths and do what you need to do. They can deal with their own fallout."

"And that will stop them?" She tensed in his embrace. "I don't know."

"I do." Jinx sat up. He rifled his fingers through his hair, then across his forehead. "They've controlled the narrative this long. Now they don't because you know what they're doing. That takes their power."

"So I can work again?"

"We insist, and not just for our benefit." Zephyr caressed her hip. "You're good at what you do and shouldn't be held back because someone made poor financial decisions or because someone else can't keep his ego or hands in check."

"Ditto." Jinx sighed. "Don't we have a scene to play?"

"We did." Her eyes glittered. "You came home too late."

"Did you play without me?" He gently swatted her backside.

"No." She shook her head. "By the time we got undressed, I couldn't keep my eyes open."

"I hate to admit it, but she's right and I had the same issue." Jinx situated his hand between her legs. "We waited for you."

"Then why don't we play? It's time we blew off some steam." And ended up satisfied. "Do you wish to play, girl?"

She grinned. "I do."

Then it was time to satisfy everyone.

Chapter Twelve

Onyx practically vibrated with excitement and anticipation. Every time she got to scene, she loved it, but knowing she'd be scening with Jinx and Zephyr never ceased to please her. What did they want to do? How would they make her scream? Make her beg? Didn't matter. She wanted to do it all.

"Up." Zephyr patted the bed. "On your knees."

"Yes, Sir." She scrambled to the middle of the bed and shrugged out of the shirt. The chilly air swirled around her and her nipples beaded. She clasped her hands together at the small of her back. Anticipation flowed through her veins.

"Good girl." Jinx left the mattress and grabbed a silk robe from the armchair. He swathed himself in the crimson fabric, then folded his arms.

She bit back a shiver. She loved when he and Zephyr exuded power. "Thank you, Sir." She bowed her head and waited for the next command.

Zephyr remained in bed. "I want your hands behind your head. Lace your fingers together."

"Yes, Sir." She did as told. "Thank you, Sir." She spread her knees, giving him access to her pussy. She had to be soaked by now.

"Good." Jinx opened a drawer. "I've got a pretty for you."

She couldn't see what he'd taken from the drawer, but she heard the clunk of the wood closing. She focused on the sheet. What did he have?

"These are for you." Jinx stood before her. His cock tented the front of his robe as he leaned forward. "Breathe for me."

She whimpered as the jingle of the tiny bells echoed in the room. The metal clips shimmered in the light. She tried to memorize every detail of the toys. Thin little fingers came out from the barrel and bells chimed on the other end. She sucked in a ragged breath as he affixed the clip to her nipple. The little fingers bit deep, but spread the pain out. It wasn't like with alligator clips with the instant burn. This was different and beautiful. "Thank you, Sir." She whimpered again as the second clip was affixed to her nipple.

The bells jingled as she moved. Was she supposed to be quiet? She wasn't sure.

"God, that's gorgeous." Zephyr tugged lightly on one of the clips. "Feels good?"

"Yes." She couldn't think straight. Damn. She should answer better. "Thank you, Sirs. Please? May I have another?" That made no sense, but whatever. How was she supposed to be coherent in this position? The pain morphed into pleasure in seconds. She wished she could touch herself.

Just to find orgasm.

But she wanted to wait for them.

"Hands on the bed." Jinx curled his fingers under her chin. "Show me your ass, girl."

The bells jingled again as she switched positions. She flattened her hands on the bed and arched her back, waving her butt at him. The clips pulled on her breasts. She loved the extra pain.

"You need another pretty." Zephyr left the bed and strode nearly nude across the room. His boxer briefs clung to his muscled frame. The material pulled tight across his backside. She watched him out of the corner of her eye as he opened a drawer. The same one Jinx had used? Could be. She hadn't gone through the room to find out what they'd secreted there.

Zephyr withdrew a bottle of lube and a clear glass plug. *Holy fuck.* She couldn't wait to have the plug in her body. She spread her legs and exhaled. "Thank you, Sir." She trembled as Zephyr opened the bottle. The tiny snick sent shockwaves through her. He slid chilly lube over her asshole, then speared into her body with one finger. She groaned at the impaling.

How could one man…no, two…make her so crazy? She shuddered as Zephyr withdrew his finger and slid the plug into her body.

"That's so hot in you. Like we've marked you. All ours." Zephyr spread his hand over her backside. "Don't want you to get a tattoo, but we want you to be ours forever. No one else's."

She'd love that.

Jinx held a leather paddle in his hand. "Do you want to fly?"

She nodded. "Yes, Sir." She flexed her hands in the sheets. "Please, Sirs? May I have another?" She'd been conditioned to respond that way. She had to change her thinking.

"Do you want to be ours?" Jinx rounded her, moving out of her line of sight. He slapped the paddle on his hand.

She yelped. "I've been a bad girl. I need to be punished. Will you punish me, Sirs? Make me cry out. Make me fly."

"Good girl." Zephyr stood before her. "Answer me. Do you want to belong to us?" He pushed her hair from her face.

She hadn't even taken most of the pins from her tresses. She'd slept in her hairdo and had to look like a disaster.

"You haven't answered us." Jinx brought the paddle down on her ass.

The streak of pain resonated through her. She yelped, then dug her toes into the mattress. "Thank you, Sirs. I love it. May I have another?"

"You'll get another." Jinx spanked her again. "Answer, girl. Do you want to be ours?"

"Yes." She gasped as she rocked forward from the third spank. "I want to belong to you." She bunched the sheet in her hands. The rest of her words were gone. The pleasure outweighed the pain, but it also made thinking impossible.

"Girl." Zephyr moved her hair off her face. "Are you okay? How do you feel?"

"Like I'm flying." She wanted one of them in her body. One of them to fuck her. She needed it. "Please, Sirs. I want to be yours and want you to use me." Not like she'd been used by others. She wanted them to make her fly higher.

"Good girl." Jinx stopped spanking her and slid the paddle over her ass. He smoothed the leather over her abused backside. "You make us happy."

"You make us very happy. We wouldn't have chosen you if we didn't feel that way. You're a gem. You deserve better," Zephyr said. He kept moving her hair from her face. "You please me. Please Jinx. You're our girl and we're not letting go. Not letting anyone push you around."

She sighed as bliss washed over her. Not just from their words, but the toys, words and excitement of the moment. "Thank you, Sirs." She almost said she loved them, but didn't. It was too soon. She didn't trust her own feelings yet.

Zephyr shoved his underwear down his thighs, exposing his cock. He didn't have to say a word. She knew what to do. She leaned forward and opened her mouth. She took him to the back of her throat in seconds. Power and desire rocketed through her. She bobbed her head, building into a steady rhythm to please him.

"I fucking love that." Jinx paddled her once more, pushing her hard onto Zephyr's cock. "I want to be inside you. Want Zeph inside you, too. Marking you. Making you ours. Not a pawn, but our queen. Our girl."

That's what she wanted, too. She kept going, pumping on his cock and loving every second. She adjusted around Zephyr as Jinx settled behind her. He held onto her hips.

"No, I want you on top." Jinx nudged her. He stretched out beside her on the bed. "On me."

"Do it." Zephyr caressed her cheek. "I want that, too."

She let go of his cock with a pop, then licked her lips. "Yes, Sirs. Thank you, Sirs." She moved over Jinx, the bells ringing as she crawled on top of him. She straddled his lap and met Jinx's gaze. The passion and love in his eyes spurred her on. She reached between her legs and guided him into her body. As she slid down on his shaft, she gasped. The stretching and burn as she adjusted to the plug in her ass and Jinx in her pussy were almost more than she could handle. She blinked, then rested her hands on his belly. Should she clasp her hands behind her back? He hadn't told her what to do.

Jinx slid his hands over hers. "Look at me. Breathe."

She wanted to, but her brain didn't want to cooperate. As she bounced on his lap, the clips pulled at her nipples. The bells jangled. A shiver raced through her. She'd never be able to hold back the orgasm at this rate.

"Come here." Jinx tugged her forward. He slid his arms around her and held onto her hips as he guided her up and down on his dick. "Zeph needs to be in on this. Are you ready to let him?"

She nodded, unable to speak. She huddled against his chest, appreciating the change in position. The clips didn't pull on her nipples so much, but they bit in a little deeper. She focused on Jinx as he pushed into her. His words, soft and kind, helped.

"Look at me and breathe. You're our gem," Jinx said. He splayed his hands on her hips. "Breathe."

She gasped as the chilly lube slid down her ass crack, then gulped as the plug was removed. She expected Zephyr to ram right into her body, but instead, she didn't feel the movement of him on the bed. *Where is he?*

The bed shifted and warmth centered on her spine. A kiss. Zephyr feathered his mouth along her back to the swell of her hip. She whimpered as Zephyr grasped her ass. She couldn't see him enter her, but she felt the blunt head of his erection nudge against her hole.

"Breathe and bear down on him. Relax." Jinx stopped thrusting and tucked a lock of her hair behind her ear. "You're pleasing us. Very much, girl."

She needed to hear those words. She grasped at his shoulders, unintentionally digging her nails into Jinx's skin as Zephyr pushed into her. He moved slowly, giving her time to accept him into her body. Her nerve endings sizzled and her thoughts scattered. With both men invading her, she flew.

She'd wanted to fly higher and they'd delivered. Every cell in her body floated. The best she could do was hold on while Jinx and Zephyr pumped into her. They moved perfectly together, when one nearly pulled out, the other pushed in. She'd never been so thoroughly owned and loved at one time in her life.

"Fuck," Jinx bit out. "Can't hold this one back. Fuck. I gotta come." His cock throbbed deep within her pussy. She swore he touched her everywhere from within. She shivered with him and matched his lazy smile with one of her own.

She wasn't going to argue with him. The orgasm building in her rushed to its zenith. She panted as they continued to fuck her. She teetered on the edge of coming apart.

"Jesus H. Christ." Zephyr growled as he moved faster. Skin slapped against skin. The sound of their excitement rippled through the room. Zephyr slapped her ass. "Come with us. Holy fuck." This time, he surged into her and his hot seed filled her body. His breath tickled along her back. He added a couple more thrusts before slowing.

She didn't need the command. She'd been so close she could taste the climax. A groan ripped from her throat. She fell right over the edge into oblivion and came. Nothing else mattered and the world evaporated around her. She simply sprawled between her men, allowing them to use her and she loved every second. This was where she belonged.

When she wasn't in front of the camera, she was meant to be with Jinx and Zephyr. They'd called her their girl. They'd claimed they wanted her. She was their gem. Maybe they could love her. Maybe they could be the ones to turn her world around. They'd changed it for the better already. They'd shown her respect and appreciation.

How could she not want to be with them?

Did they love her?

Sure felt like it was possible. Men didn't use such terms as they did without having some sort of love there.

"Fuck me." Zephyr rested against her back, bracing himself on his hands. "You wring me out."

She had no words and simply enjoyed being between them.

"At least I'm not the only one who feels worn out." Jinx kissed her. "You're electric."

"Thank you," she managed.

Zephyr withdrew, then collapsed beside Jinx on the bed. "It's a good way to be wrung out." He reached for her. "Come here."

She slid off Jinx, but instead of stretching out with them, she sat up. Zephyr leaned forward and sucked on her nipple, then carefully eased the clip off her battered skin. The sensitivity remained and she moaned.

"Let me in on that." Jinx matched Zephyr's actions and removed the other clip. While Zephyr continued to lap at her nipple, Jinx sucked on the other. She allowed herself to move and cupped each man's head. Other than having them both inside her, this was one of the sexiest things she'd ever experienced.

"Yes, Sirs." She caressed each man's head. The softness of their hair and the tenderness of their touch pleased her. "Thank you, Sirs. I don't deserve your kindness, but I love it. I love you." She should've kept those words to herself, but she'd let them slip. Now she didn't care. She'd been honest and worn her heart on her sleeve. If they wanted to accept her heart, they would. She'd been set free in their tender bonds and she never wanted to leave.

"You do?" Jinx cupped her breast as he helped her onto her back. "Good thing. I'm fond of you, too."

Fond. She wanted to hear the word love in return, but she'd take it. Maybe he didn't believe in love.

"He's being modest." Zephyr caressed her belly. He stretched out beside her and traced circles around her navel. "I love you, too. We didn't choose you on a whim. You're our girl."

"And we're not letting go." Jinx dragged the blanket back over them and held onto her.

Zephyr tangled up to her left while Jinx did the same on her right. She tucked her head in the crook of Jinx's neck. "I appreciate it, Sirs."

Zephyr sighed. "It'll all get worked out, but you're ours and we don't intend to lose. You're not just another sweet smile with a body that goes on forever…and those legs… You're a vibrant, loving, tender woman with a huge heart and we're honored that you chose us, too."

"Rest, now, sweetheart. We've got you," Jinx whispered.

Her heart leapt. They'd given her respect but dignity, too. They'd given her hope. She'd never known men who could be so honest. She didn't want to let go.

She'd found home for as long as it'd last.

Chapter Thirteen

Jinx checked his watch. In the three days since he and Zephyr had the scene with Onyx, they hadn't heard a peep out of Keifer. Zephyr claimed he'd heard from Xavier, but hadn't gone into detail. He would've liked some idea of what was happening, but he had to trust his friend.

Onyx stepped out of the bedroom and adjusted her blouse. "Will this work?"

"It will." He swept his gaze over her after he'd spoken. He didn't have to look at her to know she was put together. The woman had style and when given the chance to show it, she could sparkle.

"I haven't done this in so long." She laughed and the nervous sound filled his ears. "It's been years."

"You'll be fine." He walked with her through the house to the staged living room. The beauty of having the extra home meant they could use it for advertising on a much cheaper basis than having to rent a space.

The photographer and videographer were at work behind the tools of their trade. A woman adjusted the boom mic and another man gestured Onyx over.

"I need to touch up your makeup. Won't take much. Did you do it yourself?" the makeup artist asked. "Have you had practice?"

"I have." She straightened her shoulders and stole a glance at Jinx before allowing the makeup artist to work.

"I'll be over here." Jinx moved to the edge of the room, plenty out of the way. He sat on one of the barstool chairs to watch her work. He probably should've asked her before he decided to look on. Maybe she didn't want him around.

He scanned the script she'd been given. There wasn't much to say and the man she'd interact with, one of the groundskeepers, Mike, did quite a bit of the talking this time around. They'd used Mike before because he'd been good at delivering the lines.

"Ready?"

At the videographer's direction, Jinx glanced up from the words on his phone. He watched in awe as Onyx shifted into the role of the woman in charge. She knew when to smile, when to nod and how to interact with Mike. Like she was born to do this job.

She posed with Mike, making it look like she couldn't wait to make a purchase. Within an hour, she'd handled posing for the photographs and delivered the lines for the ad space five times over.

She had a certain poise about her and Jinx admired her skill. He liked to take photos and paint, but he hated being in front of the camera. Hated having to speak to groups. The very idea of having to be the center of attention made his stomach churn.

She seemed to take it all in stride.

"We're done for now. I'd like to have her change clothes and switch Mike for Dickie. We could do some exterior shots. What do you think?" the photographer asked. "Mr. Collins? Ms. Power?"

Jinx liked hearing her referred to as his equal. "I'm fine with it, if she is." He didn't mind taking the production outside.

"Sure." She smiled, then bowed her head and strode from the room.

Jinx paused. She didn't have to defer. He left his chair and abandoned his phone on the counter and hurried to the bedroom. "What's wrong?"

"What?" She'd eased the button down off her shoulders. "What's wrong?"

"That's what I asked you." He stilled her hands. "You bowed your head."

She half-shrugged. "I did, but it's... I'm sorry."

"It's been ingrained in you, hasn't it?" He held onto her fingers. "You have power here, Ms. Power. You can call some shots. Not because you're sleeping with me, but because you have a good eye for what's happening. I noticed how you adjusted your stance before the videographer could speak and how you knew where to put your hands. You're a natural in front of the camera. Don't forget that."

"I don't want to overstep." Her façade of calm fell for a moment. "They're in charge. I'm just the eye candy."

"That's minimizing your talent." He cupped her cheek. "Don't do that. You're good at what you do and could even be the director. Hell, you'll probably end up doing that eventually. You're good, babe. Remember that."

She sighed. "You have a lot of faith in me."

"Because I've seen you work. You're good." He brushed his thumb across her cheek. "You can't let me down."

"Thanks," she whispered. "I should change."

"You should. And twist your hair up. Change it a little." He kissed her. "Oh, and don't forget that I love you."

"Thank you, Sir." She stayed close to him another moment. "I love you, too."

He paused in the doorway. She was a sight to behold and he was lucky to have her in his life.

She held up the lavender blouse, then clutched it to her chest. "I have a request."

"Sure." He'd do just about whatever she wanted.

"Can we get a few more of my things from the apartment? My photos and more of my clothes? I like what you've bought me, but they're mine and I'd like to have them back."

"We'll do that when you're done and I'll take you myself." He refused to let her go alone. "Will that work?"

"It will. Thank you." She exhaled and seemed to relax.

"I'll be outside, but I'll find you when you're done." He left her to change and fix her hair for the second set of photos. He did have faith in her and knew the ads would be dynamic.

Jinx headed back to the counter to retrieve his phone. The screen flashed, then darkened. He groaned before picking up the device. While the camera crews moved outside to the front of the house, he wandered out behind the workers to watch the action, but also to keep out of the way.

He checked the notification. A text from Zephyr. At least it wasn't something worse. He inched out of the range of the mics before he called his best friend back. "You screamed?"

"I did," Zephyr said when he answered. "I'm surprised you returned my call this quickly. I figured you'd be busy ordering people around."

"Don't have to. She's got this in hand." He kept one eye on her while she went through the motions of the script. "She's a natural, not that we doubted her."

"Good. I hoped she'd excel."

"She has," he replied. "I told her she had a future in directing if she desired it. She knows what to do and she'll make us look good. Even better that she's not only our secret weapon, but our greatest asset."

"She is. I haven't figured out how we're going to make this permanent, but I'm working on the contract. I'm also working on a set of rings. She deserves that at least."

"She does." He agreed wholeheartedly. "I like it."

"But that's not why I called."

He should've guessed. "Okay?"

"You didn't read my text, did you?"

"Nope. Just saw you'd called."

"I heard from Xavier."

His stomach clenched. "Okay?"

"The transfer went through and we bankrolled a new playroom," Zephyr said. "The cash is in Xavier's hands, by way of the corporation, but as far as Keifer knows, it's in his."

"And?" He held his breath, waiting for the answer.

"To be honest, it seems to be going the way I wanted, but I don't trust him. He's called me to let me know he's happy with the way things are proceeding, but it's not enough," Zephyr said. "A cool million isn't enough."

"What the ever-loving fuck?" He didn't mind spending the money. The amount wasn't important as long as they had Onyx out of the club. Jesus Christ, he just wanted her to be safe. But this dickhead thought he could con them out of more money. No doubt he thought he deserved more of a payday.

"I know." Zephyr paused. "He won't get another cent. Xavier and I agreed on the amount, which he said was more than enough. Keifer believes we owe another half a mil. The only way he'll allow her freedom is if we cough up more money."

"The hell we will," he snapped. "Let me guess. Nacin is now sniffing around, too?"

"Would you believe it, you're right?" Zephyr chuckled. "He wanted to know what we're doing with her. He suggested we keep her out of sight."

"When did the ass say that?"

"When he called me half an hour ago," Zephyr said. "Keifer must've given him my number."

"He can fuck himself right the fuck off." He hated being this angry. Swearing wasn't a good look for a businessman, but damn it. This bullshit had to stop. "She's not going into hiding because he's afraid she'll prove he's a piece of shit."

"I agree, but we need to be smart about this."

"I know." He tamped down his fury. "She wants to get her stuff from her apartment. I'm going with her so she won't have to go alone, but also so she's not in the line of fire. I don't trust that either will leave her alone, no matter how much money we give them. Nacin fumes because he can't keep her silenced because he knows he fucked up. Keifer wants her under him so he can bankroll his misfortunes. It's a load of shit and she's not having that on her back any longer."

"No, she's not. I've got the situation with Nacin and Keifer in hand. You just worry about getting her where she needs to go," Zephyr said. "This has to end and it's ending today."

"Good." He hung up on Zephyr and slammed his phone into his pocket. The nerve of people to use others for their own gain. He knew fear when he saw it. The fear in Onyx's eyes that she'd be abused again. The panic in Nacin's actions that he'd be outed for his bad behavior. The worry in Keifer's whole being that he'd lose his income. Zephyr was right — it all had to end.

Onyx shouldn't be scared. She had talent and deserved to enjoy it.

"Sir?" Onyx strode up to him. She wore a wrap around her shoulders and she'd pulled her hair into a low ponytail. "You look like you're going to tear someone or something apart."

"I'm irked." He sighed and attempted to tamp down his frustration, but it was no use. "Keifer wants more money for your freedom and Nacin demands that you stay out of sight. They can both fuck off."

"Maybe I should go back," she said. "I'm more trouble than I'm worth."

"No." He'd had enough of this. "You might not believe you've got value after what they've done to you, but I don't see it that way. Neither does Zephyr. You just owned that advertising session. Hell, you should've been running it. You knew what to do."

"Sir." She held tight to the wrap. "I can back down."

"No." This time, he did release some of his frustration. She wasn't the problem. "I'm tired of fighting with them over something they created. Don't molest anyone and you won't have to worry about them staying out of the way. Don't abuse anyone and you won't have to deal with the repercussions of your actions. Don't gamble and fuck your money away, then it won't be so important for you to get more cash. Don't use people to fucking pay your bills because you're an ass who can't handle money."

She inched backward and nodded. "I'm sorry."

"You don't have to be sorry." He shook his head. "That's just it. You're the one apologizing, not them. You're the one capitulating and they're benefiting. That's bullshit."

"It is." She tensed. "I…"

"If you tell me you'll leave or you'll give in, I won't have it. You're a strong woman, but you've been kicked too many times. Zeph and I are trying to be a shield. Let us."

A tear slipped down her cheek. "I'm sorry."

He reached for her and enfolded her in his embrace. "I'm angry because they've been despicable for so long and you've had to let it happen. They're lower than low." He petted her hair. "They're afraid of what you'll say because you've got power. We're here to help you use it."

"I will." She held onto his shirt. "I'm tired."

"I know you are."

"I don't have much fight in me."

"That's why you've got us."

"Don't let me go."

"Never." He kissed her temple and clung to her. She'd found a way to melt the ice around his heart. "You matter to us more than any award, money or treasure." He hadn't planned on falling for her this fast, but he also couldn't imagine his life without her. She added a dimension to his existence. Added color to the shades of gray. Became the new melody played over the tune he'd created with Zephyr. She complemented them, helping them to find the balance they'd been searching for.

After what seemed like an eternity, but was probably only a few minutes, he loosened his grasp a bit. "Why don't you change into something you want to wear and we'll head to the apartment? I'll text Zeph to let him know where we are."

"I'd like that." She kissed him on the cheek. "I'll never be able to repay you."

"Don't need to." He held onto her hand a bit longer. "Be you and be our girl. We'll draw up a contract we all approve of and make this permanent—if you want. We want to spoil you rotten."

"You already do." She finally smiled. "I love it, even if it's too much."

"That's our job, to be too much." He didn't care. He loved to give his lovers more than they could ever dream of having.

"I'll change. Where will you be?"

"Hot on your heels." He winked and let go of her. As she walked away, he watched her butt as she took each step. She had a great ass. His mouth watered and he wished he could take her right there in the bedroom. There were too many people milling around. The idea of being caught did spur him on, but not enough to make her uncomfortable.

He chased after her all the way into the house, then stopped in the corridor outside of the bedroom. He texted Zephyr, letting him know where they were going. He'd have Calvin drive them and he'd stay with her as she packed.

She'd done enough on her own. Now she had him and Zephyr in her corner. They wouldn't let her down.

By the time he finished sending the texts and getting the SUV arranged, Onyx emerged from the bedroom.

"I forgot how much makeup and how many clothes are involved in a shoot. They've got enough outfit pairings for me to make a dozen ad spots." She closed the door behind me. "How did you manage to get that many garments in such a short period of time?"

"We have connections and the boutiques downtown like to help when they get a little business their way." He shrugged. "We wanted you to look your best and the budget isn't an object."

"I know." She slid her arm around his forearm. "The only thing missing from this shoot was the catering table."

"Do you want something to eat?" He should've thought of that before now. "You're probably famished."

"I'm fine." She bumped shoulders with him as they left the house. "Hold on." She let go of him and thanked the various crew members. She offered compliments easily and spent a moment with each person, sharing a short conversation. The ease with which she gave them her attention amazed him. He knew the importance of being kind, but she made it into an art.

She finished speaking to the crew, then returned to his side. "Thanks."

"Thank you. That was the best thing you could've done," he said. "I should've joined you, but I was in awe."

"There's something special to be said about being kind to the crew. Not just to suck up, but because it's the right thing to do." She walked with him out to the waiting SUV. "Is this our chariot?"

"Complete with a driver." He opened the door for her. "Let's get your stuff so we can come home and show our appreciation."

She shivered and grinned. "I can't wait."

Neither could he.

Chapter Fourteen

Onyx rode with Jinx to her apartment. For the first time in her life, things were going right. No, this wasn't the first time. When she'd met Jinx and Zephyr, the course changed for the better. She'd found her princes and they treated her like a queen. She'd been so lucky. At the time, she'd thought her life was over. She was being used at a club and living, essentially, in the darkness. If she hadn't been put in that position, she never would've met them. Wouldn't have been given the chance to add the color back into her existence.

She snuggled against Jinx. She loved the way he and Zephyr touched her. Even when they brought her pain, that delicious hurt gave her the strongest pleasure.

When they reached the apartment building, she shuddered. She hadn't been back to her home in nearly two weeks, but they'd been the best weeks with Zephyr and Jinx. Part of her didn't want to go in. Why go back to the shit she'd come from? But she needed to get this over with. She had to return and clean out the place.

Someone else could have the apartment and maybe make it the home it was always meant to be.

"You okay?" Jinx asked. He grasped her hand. "I've got you."

"I know you do." And Calvin was in the front seat if they needed him, too. She forced a smile. The apartment wasn't a bad place, but not the best one. "I want to get this over with."

"Then let's do that." He followed her out of the car. "If you want, I can have a moving crew come in and box your things up, then move them to the staging house so you can go through it and figure out what you want to toss and keep."

"I'd like that." She fumbled with her keys. As she stepped up to the front door, another shudder ran through her. Something felt off. "I want to go home."

"What?" He stepped between her and the door. "What's wrong?"

"I can't explain what I feel, but something isn't right. I can't go in there." She dropped her keys.

"Did you hear from someone?" He grasped her by the shoulders. "Did he contact you?"

"No." She froze. She understood what he was doing. He wasn't trying to scare her. He'd shifted into control mode. He had to be feeling helpless and unsure of what to do. Not that she knew how to handle this, either.

He let go. "I'm sorry." The muscle in his jaw twitched and he shook his head. "I'm sorry. I want to fix this and I can't."

"I know." She balled her hands. "I'm afraid to go back there because I don't want to go back to my old life. I don't want to think about the shit I've been through. I just want to move forward, but I have to face my past. I can't ignore it because I have to get out of lease. I can't let you do it for me. Eventually, I'll have to sign the paperwork."

"You don't have to do it all today."

She leveled her shoulders. "No, but if I don't do this, I'll never do it and I won't be able to prove to myself I'm strong."

"This isn't the way to prove you are. Sweetheart, you've got strength people can't fathom and you show it every day. This is going through the motions." He caressed her inner wrist. "Let's go home."

"No. I need to do this. I need to close this chapter." She held onto his hand, but unlocked the door to the building. Once in the foyer, she checked her mailbox. The little cubby overflowed with letters and envelopes. She emptied the slot and handed the mail to Jinx. "I'll go through this later."

"Sure." He arranged the letters, getting them into some sort of order.

She gestured to the elevator. "I'd use the stairs, but you never know what you'll encounter there."

"What…I don't want to know, do I?" he asked. He kept up with her. "That bad?"

She sighed as the doors opened. "If you can imagine it'd be in the stairwell, it's there. If it's something you think might be too fantastical and gross to be there, it's probably there. One time, someone left a blowup doll between the third and fourth floors. Why you'd abandon such a thing in the stairwell, I don't know."

"I'm speechless." He stood with her in the elevator car. "Honestly, I have no words."

"Neither did I when I saw it." She pressed the button for the fifth floor, then waited for the car to ascend. Her heart hammered. "Would it be bad if I asked you to stay outside? Don't go in?"

"I'd prefer to be with you. I don't care what state the apartment's in. I'm more worried about your safety." He braced his hand on the wall as the car lurched to a stop.

"Then wash your hands." She left the car first and headed down the hallway to her door. "I don't know what's been against that wall."

"Lovely." He stood behind her as she unlocked her apartment door.

She nudged the door open and stepped inside. Before Jinx could follow her, a force mashed the barrier closed. She yelped, turning to grasp the door. She hadn't left any windows open. When she moved, something yanked her arm.

"Onyx?" Jinx pounded on the door, the sound thundering in the room. "Let me in. What's going on?"

Hell if she knew. She tugged against the force holding her, but ended up face to face with Keifer. Her breath wrenched from her chest.

"Thought you could do this, huh?" he snarled.

She wanted to speak, to scream, but no sound came out.

"Onyx, is the door stuck? I can't open it," Jinx said. He thumped against it. "Let me in."

"Don't you dare say a word." Keifer twisted her arm. "Don't you dare."

She swore she didn't breathe. She allowed him to yank her away from the door to the bedroom. While he manhandled her, she scanned the space for anything to help her get free.

"Thought you could get away from me." He slammed her into the wall of her bedroom. "Thought you could scam me. Thought you'd found someone who's smarter than me." He rammed his arm into her throat, while pressing something into her abdomen.

"Don't do this," she managed. "Don't."

"Don't do this? You took everything from me. My income, my place at the club, my friendship with my mentor. They fucking fired me from Sixxes." He pushed harder into her belly. "I lost my job because of you. Lost my money."

"You used me," she whispered. "You lied to me so you could get out of your damn debts."

"You owed me."

"For what?" She struggled in his grasp. When she moved, she saw what he'd pushed into her abdomen. *A gun. Fuck.* She swore she heard Jinx in the other room, but she couldn't make out what he said or make a sound to get his attention.

"Nacin won't speak to me. I idolized him and you made him hate me. You lied about what he did to you, ruined him and ruined me." He slapped her, making her ears ring.

She blinked as the pain radiated through her skull. She hadn't lied about anything. Hadn't ruined anyone. They'd done that to themselves.

"You were supposed to see me as your savior. Supposed to let me handle this, but you didn't. Couldn't. You ruined everything." He slammed her into the wall again. "If I can't have you, then no one will."

An explosion ran in her ears. She wanted to make noise, but no sound came out and everything seemed to be moving in slow motion. She coughed.

Keifer's eyes widened and his mouth formed an O. The color seemed to drain from his face. "What have I done?"

She had no idea, but she slumped to the floor. When she looked at her hands, red stained her fingers. She managed to shift her gaze back to Keifer, her world fuzzed, then slowly turned black.

"I'm sorry," Keifer said. "Baby, I'm sorry."

She closed her eyes. Everything hurt and nothing made sense, but she allowed the darkness to swallow her. Maybe it was time to let go.

Jinx pounded on the door. He smashed the wood with his fists, not getting an answer from her. He heard muffled words from the other side and his anger flared. What in the hell was going on?

A pop resounded from the other side and he froze. He knew that sound—a gunshot. Fucking balls. She'd been sad, but enough to commit...he refused to think the worst. But if she had, then he'd get the fuck in there. He noticed the fire hose and axe in the cabinet. He kicked in the glass, triggering the alarm in the building. Despite the thundering noise, he slammed the axe into the door. He hacked until he broke through.

A woman rushed down the hallway. "Is there a fire?"

"Call the police. Someone's been shot." He continued to drive the axe into the door until he tore a large enough hole to open it.

Another pop echoed in the apartment and stopped him in his tracks. "Onyx?" Without bothering to protect himself, he barged into the bedroom. His heart nearly exploded. Keifer lay on the floor in a heap, blood pouring from his temple.

Onyx sat slumped against the wall. Her eyes were closed and she held onto her abdomen. Blood stained her hands and her shirt. Her head rested against her shoulder with her lips slightly parted.

"No, no, no, no," he said and scrambled across the room to her. "Onyx. Stay with me." He held her in one arm and fumbled with his phone in the other. He dialed nine-one-one, then helped her onto her back on the floor.

"Nine-one-one, what's the nature of your emergency?" the operator asked.

"I need police and EMS at the Glade Building. Room five-sixty-two. Two gunshot victims. Please, hurry." He wasn't sure how he'd been able to sound so coherent, but he'd do whatever it took to keep Onyx alive.

"Are they breathing? I've got help on the way. Can you tell if they're breathing?" the operator asked.

"Yes." He detected a faint pulse in her throat. "I can't tell with the other victim, but the female victim does have a pulse." Tears thickened in his voice and he rocked with her in his arms, not wanting to let her go. He tucked the phone between his shoulder and ear, then grabbed a piece of clothing from the floor to push against her wound. "She's bleeding from her abdomen. Please!"

"I've got help on the way. The other victim isn't breathing?" the operator asked.

"I can't tell. He's across the room."

"Can you check?"

No. He growled, but focused on Keifer. "He doesn't appear to be moving. I think he shot my girlfriend." He spotted the gun in Keifer's hand. *Dear fucking God.* The asshole must've shot them both.

The sounds of radio scratching, thumping on the floor and a scream filled his ears. He glanced up to see the EMS team rush into the room.

"She's breathing, but it's faint." He allowed the team to move her and take over. Jinx crawled out of the way, stopped by the police. He'd cooperate in any way they wanted. He abandoned his phone on the floor.

"We'll need you to come with us." The officer guided him to the living room. "What's your connection to the victims?"

"Onyx Power is my girlfriend. Keifer, the man on the floor, is one of the managers at the club, Sixxes." He ran through the highlights of the story between Onyx and Keifer before steering back to the scene. "I brought her here to collect her things since she's moving in with my partner, Zephyr Anderson, and I. Before I could get in the door, it was slammed in my face. She wasn't the one who slammed it. I heard muffled talking, then sobbing and a pop. When I heard the pop, I used the fire axe to slash the door open to get into the apartment. The axe is over there." He pointed to the floor.

"And what did you find when you arrived in the bedroom?"

"I found Keifer on the floor, appearing to be bleeding out. I didn't give him aid, though I probably should've, because I noticed Onyx and my focus became saving her."

As he spoke, the EMS team had Onyx on a spinal board.

"Is she going to be okay?" He wanted to chase after and stay with her. "I can't lose her."

"I'm not sure at this time, but we'll need your clothing for evidence and would like to swab your hands for traces of gunpowder." The officer directed him to the door. "We can do that at the hospital."

"Sure." As long as he could follow her, he'd be fine. Let them check him. He had nothing to hide. He cooperated with the police, joining them at the cruiser.

Calvin stood by the car. "Boss?"

"Call Zephyr. Tell him to meet us at the hospital." He allowed the officer to help him into the back of the squad car. His head swam as he rode to the hospital. The world seemed to go by in a blur and his thoughts were a mess. How had he missed Keifer being in the apartment? Why hadn't he listened to her when she'd told him she wanted to leave? He'd allowed her to be hurt. How was he going to live with himself?

Once he got to the hospital, he complied with the police. He offered over his clothes and allowed them to swab his hands. He cooperated each time they asked him to recount his story. He wasn't sure how much time had passed, but his thoughts never ventured far from Onyx. He hadn't been informed on her status.

"I'd like to see him."

Jinx knew that voice. *Zephyr. Thank God.* He sat up, tired of wearing the crummy hospital garb instead of his own clothes. The curtain moved and the officer, along with Zephyr joined him in the small space.

"You're free to go. I believe the hospital staff have some updates for you. We will be in touch, though, so thank you," the officer said, then left him alone with Zephyr.

"They thought I killed him, didn't they?" Jinx bowed his head. "I wasn't quick enough to save her from getting hurt."

"No, but no one knew he was in there." Zephyr sat beside him and offered him a bag. "Want to change?"

"Yeah." He shrugged out of the drab green hospital smock-style shirt. "I never should've...I don't know what."

"You did the best you could. He wanted to hurt her, no matter if you'd have been there or not. Knowing you were on the other side of the door probably kept him from doing something worse." Zephyr unfolded the pair of jeans. "She's stable."

"She is?" He practically whooped. "Will she be okay?"

"The initial report is that the bastard managed to miss major organs. She's bled out a lot, but between your intervention and getting her help as quickly as you did, it probably saved her life. If she'd have been there on her own, she would've bled out and might not have made it."

He switched out of the hospital pants and into his jeans. "I don't know."

"I do. We were in her path for a reason. I can't shake the guilt that I went to work today, but you were there. We intervened in her life and that's what saved her." Zephyr grasped Jinx's wrist. "She's going to be okay."

"Why can't I believe that? Why can't I unload the guilt? I can see her sitting there slumped over. Can see him lying there with that glazed look in his eyes. I'll never forget that." He zipped his jeans, then put his shoes back on. "I've got her blood on my hands." He held out his left hand. She'd just been telling him to wash up after touching the wall of the elevator, then he'd pressed the towel into her wound.

"We're going to do a lot of healing together," Zephyr said. "But we've still got each other."

"Why'd he do it?"

"From what I've gathered, he found out Xavier was onto him and learned the money wasn't coming. Somehow Nacin learned the same things and cut off the friendship. No money, no status and it must've seemed like he had nothing to live for. It's a bad cocktail and it manifested in what he did." Zephyr stared at him. "He was going to hurt someone, anyone, but she was his target. We weren't going to stop him, but we managed to intervene enough to get her to people who could save her."

He rested his hands on his hips and bowed his head. "Yeah."

"Think about it. Keifer took the coward's way out, but Nacin still won't get away with what he did, either. She's still here and can still testify against him."

"Yeah." He flexed his fingers in his pockets. Something good would come from this situation, but fuck, if he couldn't see it right now. He wouldn't until he saw her and knew she was okay.

Seeing was certainly believing.

Chapter Fifteen

Zephyr didn't blame Jinx for feeling guilty. He had plenty himself, but them feeling bad for themselves wasn't going to help her. She needed them to be strong. Besides, his anger wouldn't change anything.

"The police are handling the situation with Keifer and the other with Nacin. It's up to her to press charges, but they're investigating the claims." Zephyr moved the curtain and gestured to the nurse. "Thank you."

She accepted Jinx's garments in a laundry bag, then left them alone.

"We should head out to the waiting area." Zephyr directed Jinx from the emergency room bay to the open space beyond, then through the hospital to a quieter, dimly lit room. A woman waited on one of the couches and the televisions played home improvement shows without the sound on.

"I got in touch with her mother. Her father's been dead for years and her mother wasn't interested in speaking to her. Apparently when you don't bankroll your mother's life, you don't exist to her."

"That's fucked up," Jinx replied. "She didn't change her tune when she realized who was talking to her?"

"She did and she showed interest. Said she'd like to speak to me further. I got the impression she didn't give a shit about her daughter, unless her daughter could help fund her lifestyle. It looks like Maria Bowles married a guy who had some cash, but she burned through it." Zephyr shrugged. "If she thinks she's getting money from us, then she can forget it. I don't respect anyone who uses their child that way and only wants money."

"Yeah." Jinx sat on one of the sofas and rested his elbows on his knees, then his head in his hands.

"I know it's lot to handle." He had no idea how Jinx was still upright. "Want to close your eyes and try to rest?"

"Not until I know how she is." Jinx didn't bother to raise his head. "I need to see that she's okay."

He had to agree. He'd like an update as well.

"I thought I heard you'd come up here." A man in a suit strode up to them. "I'm Detective Holden. I'd like to get your statements concerning Mr. George Nacin, in conjunction with Lyle Keifer."

"You mean Keifer Jones?" Jinx said without looking at the officer.

"We know him as Keifer Jones," Zephyr said and stood. He shook hands with Holden. "How can we help you?"

"I know you've been through trauma, Mr. Collins, so I won't bother you as of right now, but I will need your statement concerning the incident." Holden turned his attention to Zephyr. "Can you explain to me the situation between you, Mr. Keifer, Mr. Nacin and the Norse Group, with Xavier Norse?"

"Well…" He invited the detective to sit with him and Jinx, then recounted the details as he remembered them. He tried not to leave out anything, but still be precise.

Detective Holden jotted down notes. He nodded every once in a while as Zephyr spoke. "Very good."

"Very good?" Zephyr inclined his head. "What's that mean? What's good? She's been shot, one of the guilty parties is dead…"

"Those aren't good, no." Holden put the notepad away. "This isn't the first time we've investigated this situation. Keifer's been on our radar for a while. Changing his name seems to be just the beginning. George Nacin has been on our notice for a while, as well. She's got the strongest claim against him, but she's not the only woman to come to our attention. More than fifteen women have claims against him. Some aren't as extreme as with Ms. Power, but hers is certainly one of the strongest."

"So you're going to do something about it?" Jinx asked. He finally looked at the detective. "You're going to stop him?"

"We're investigating it and turning our findings over to the district attorney. If the accusations are true, then he's got a lot to answer for." Holden stood. "I'd like to talk to Ms. Power, but I want to give her time first. This isn't going anywhere and there are others to investigate while she rests. But I will be back." He offered Zephyr his card.

"Thanks." He tucked the business card into his pocket. "We'll be in touch."

"Take care of her and yourselves. You have been through trauma and you need time to heal. Be good to each other. Be patient." Holden shook hands with Zephyr, then Jinx, before leaving them alone in the waiting room. Even the other woman had gone.

Zephyr settled beside Jinx. "At least it seems like the situation's being investigated."

"Not just the shooting." Jinx stretched his legs and leaned back in his seat, resting his head on the cushion. "I just want to see her."

"I do, too." The sooner, the better. But he wanted the doctors to do their best and take their time.

"Excuse me? Mr. Collins? Mr. Anderson?" A doctor strode up to them. "Gentlemen, I'm Doctor Reid. I'm the lead on Ms. Power's case."

"Oh." Zephyr jumped to his feet, but slapped Jinx's arm in the process. "Yes."

"The nurses thought you were still in the emergency wing." Dr. Reid half-chuckled. "It's fine that you moved. We need the space over there." He shook hands with Zephyr then Jinx.

"We were trying to get out of the way." Jinx scrubbed his hands over his face. "Do you have some updates?"

"I do." Dr. Reid folded his arms. "She's awake and requesting you. First, though, the bullet went through her abdomen, but managed to miss major organs. We were able to repair the damage and she'll make a full recovery, but she'll need some time. She lost a lot of blood and we had to give her three units before we could get to work. She's going to make a full recovery, so be kind to her. Gentle, but I think the best medicine would be you visiting her."

"I agree," Zephyr said.

Jinx nodded.

"I do have one question. We've tried to contact her next of kin, but got no answer. Have we got the wrong information?" the doctor asked.

"No. She and her mother are estranged." Zephyr sighed. "We'll handle the financial aspect of her recovery."

"I wasn't worried about that." Dr. Reid gestured to the hallway. "Let me take you to her room. Normally, I'd have one of my nursing staff escort you, but they're unfortunately stretched thin. The numbers aren't there."

"Hiring is problematic everywhere." Zephyr followed Dr. Reid down the corridor. "I'm thankful you came to speak to us."

"Yes." Jinx kept up with them. "I appreciate it as well."

"I find when the situation is as it is with Ms. Power, the doctor is truly the best messenger." Dr. Reid escorted them down the corridor. "She's not out of the anesthesia yet. Talk to her and let her know you're there. When she wakes, give her time. She might not look great right now, but she'll gain her strength soon enough."

"Understood." Jinx remained outside of the room a moment. "Fuck."

"Will you be in and out?" Zephyr asked. "Or will the nursing staff?"

"They'll be around to check on her and take her vitals. I'll leave you with her. Do you have any questions?" Dr. Reid asked.

"I don't," Jinx said. He scrubbed both hands over his face. "I'm… I need a minute."

He might not have a question, but Zephyr did. "Can you suggest counseling? I know she'll need to talk to someone after this." He watched Jinx pace. "Can you suggest some things we can do help her?"

"Mostly, be strong for her. This is going to be tough and she's going to hurt. She had a foreign object rip through her body and cause destruction. She'll come back from it, but it'll take time. Be the rock she'll need and take care of the three of you."

He stared at the doctor. "You're not shocked we're three?" He'd expected a lecture.

"Nothing surprises me. I see people tear each other up all day long and see the worst in people. It's refreshing to see happy endings and makes me question less what it takes for people to be that kind of happy. If this is what makes you all who you are, then by all means. Why not do what makes you happy? I'll leave you to be with her and I'll check in on her later after my rounds." The doctor shook hands with him, then walked away.

Zephyr stopped at the doorway. When he looked into her room, she appeared to be asleep. So fragile, too. Like an angel. His heart ached. He'd never totally get over the guilt of not being there for her when she'd been shot, but he was here now. So was Jinx.

"I don't know if I can do this." Jinx flexed his hands. "Zeph."

"We've been through worse. I know it sucks. She's the one we've been waiting for, so we can't give up now. We give everything we need for her to get back to one hundred percent. It'll be okay," he said. He grasped Jinx's shoulders. "We're all in this together."

"I know."

"It's going to get tougher, especially if she's called to testify against Nacin. If this goes down the way I expect it will, she'll have to face a lot of crap before it's over. If you're going to give up, then you're not the man I know." He stared at Jinx. "The man I know doesn't quit on those he loves."

"I won't." Jinx nodded. "Thanks. I needed to hear that."

"I know." He could use the words directed at him, too, but he'd worry about that later. He followed Jinx into the hospital room. Seeing her hooked up to so many tubes and machines stole his breath. The fragility appeared worse even worse up close. The circles under her eyes were darker and her skin ashen. She wasn't dead, but certainly weak. He wanted to caress her and prove to himself, despite the beeping of the machines, that she was alive.

Zephyr grabbed one of the chairs and dragged it to her bedside. Jinx sat on her other side. She needed their strength flanking her. They'd have to move when the nurses came in, but they'd worry about that later.

Seemed like he kept having to say them to himself.

Didn't matter.

He wanted to touch her hand, but with the IV, he worried he'd hurt her.

"Hi," she whispered. She didn't open her eyes and barely moved, but she'd spoken. The noises from the machine were so loud, compared to her thin voice.

He met Jinx's gaze for a split-second, then turned his attention to her. "Hi, sweetheart."

"I'm sorry," she managed. "I made a mess."

"Don't." He slid her hand into his. "Don't you dare apologize or take the blame for what happened. This isn't something you've done wrong or anything you could've controlled."

"We're just glad you're still here," Jinx said. "Glad you came back to us. I'm not sure we could've gone on without you."

"Did I leave you?" She finally opened her eyes, just a bit. "I tried to scream..."

"You don't have to talk to us about it." Jinx stroked her thigh. "It's okay. We're not going anywhere. Just rest."

"I think I will." She tipped her head a fraction of an inch. "What happened to him? Did they catch him?"

"He's in custody." He wasn't sure how to tell her the truth. Zephyr sighed. "He's dead."

She opened her eyes wider. "What?"

He glanced over at Jinx a moment, then shook his head. "Yeah."

"When I broke down the door and got into the apartment, he was already on the floor," Jinx said. "He can't hurt you any longer."

"He's dead?" She grasped Zephyr's hand. "I just remember he kept pushing a gun to my belly. He kept saying that I'd ruined everything." Tears slid down her cheeks and her machines beeped.

Zephyr scooted back, but kept hold of her hand and anticipated the nurses would come in to check on her. "You need to rest. There will be time to talk about this later."

"No," she replied. "I want to get this out of my head right now. He's dead and I'm not. I want to talk."

One of the nurses came in. "How are we doing? You're getting worked up." She adjusted the drip, then the machine. "Stressed out?"

"May I talk to the police?" Onyx asked. "I want to make my statement."

"I'll let them know." The nurse left almost as quickly as she'd arrived.

"Sweetheart?" Zephyr leaned in close again. He held onto her fingers, his touch tender, to keep from hurting her. "Are you sure?"

"I am." She offered a weak smile. "I learned something when I was standing there."

"What'd you learn?" Jinx asked and mirrored Zephyr's position. "We're listening."

She rubbed the top of Zephyr's hand with her thumb. At the same time, she hung onto Jinx's fingers with her other hand. Like they both gave her strength. They built her up. "I thought I was a weak woman. Thought I'd never be able to stand up to the bullies. When he yanked me into that room, I had two choices. I could either collapse and let him win or I could stand up for myself. I'd let everyone else push me around from the moment I collided with Nacin and had him threaten me. Why am I giving him power? Why give Keifer power?" she asked, her voice a bit stronger. "I will not back down. They need to pay for what they did to me."

"Keifer has to answer to someone for what he did, but it won't be in this life," Jinx said. "But he knew what he'd done and what he'd lost. He knew what he'd done and probably couldn't live with himself."

"No," she murmured. She shifted her gaze to Zephyr. "I'm tired of letting Nacin have power. No more."

"Then we're right here while you tell your story and we'll be beside you through the rest of this." He kissed the top of her hand. "You're never alone."

She sighed, then closed her eyes. "I knew you'd be honorable."

"We will." Jinx met Zephyr's gaze. "All the way."

"I trusted you." She sighed again.

"I don't know if it helps, but I did see some of the initial photos from the campaign and got to see a rough cut of the commercial," Jinx said. "The guys thought it would be something to keep my mind off my worrying. Didn't work, but I got to see what they'd produced and it's fantastic."

"Yeah?" She opened her eyes. "I'm glad. I wanted to make you both proud."

"You have." Zephyr hadn't seen the rough cuts, but he didn't care. He knew how she'd managed the campaigns with other companies. She'd been electric. "Nacin will be pissed, but I don't give a shit. He can fuck off. You need to make yourself happy and have whatever you want."

"If we can give it to you, then even better," Jinx added. "But you should rest. When the police come in, you'll need your energy."

"I know." She tried to laugh, but the sound came out brittle. "It hurts. Like the worst gut-punch. Why would someone do this?"

"Because he's a man with a problem and found the absolute wrong way to solve it," Zephyr said. "I hear footsteps and I'm guessing they're on the way. Want us to stick around?"

"If they'll let you, but I doubt they will." She inched her shoulder up in a half-shrug. "I'll be fine."

"Then we'll be outside in the hall." Zephyr let go of her hand and gestured to Jinx, who rounded the bed. "Let us know if you need us and we're here."

"You'll be right outside," she said. "Wearing a hole in the floor."

"Probably." Zephyr lingered as the officer and a nurse arrived in her room. He nodded to Holden, then the nurse and ducked into the corridor. His heart lodged in his throat. She'd be fine. He knew that to his core, but damn it. Seeing her in that shape was almost more than he could handle.

"You okay?" Jinx scrubbed his hand over the top of his head. "She's killing me in there with her strength."

"I know." He leaned against the wall and pinched the bridge of his nose. "When we can take her home, we're spoiling her rotten."

"Agreed." Jinx threw his arms around Zephyr. He hugged him a moment before letting go. "We're going to get through this. She'll be okay, we'll treat her the way she deserves and it'll work out. Right now, we've got to be strong for her so she has one less thing to worry about."

Jinx had an uncanny way of being honest and getting to the point while remaining tender. Jinx also knew how to make the moment better and take the tension away. The issues were still there, but they had time to face them because nothing had to be settled right now. They had their girl and a future with her. All they had to do was stick together.

Easy.

"How's about we finish the contract?" he asked. "And get those rings we've discussed made? I want to surprise her."

"I like the way you think." Jinx withdrew his phone from his pocket. "Let's make that design and I'll get it sent to the jeweler."

He nodded to the small alcove with a couch. He couldn't wait to get the idea in his head onto Jinx's phone screen. His suggestions and Jinx's artistic ability would be able to capture the spirit he wanted. He had the wording he wanted for the contract on his own phone. Given a few minutes and a little effort, they'd have something to present to Onyx.

Once they got her home and recovered, they'd never let her go.

Chapter Sixteen

Three months later…

Onyx walked out of the courtroom and the weight on her shoulders that had been there for the last five years finally evaporated. She'd testified against Nacin. Not just that, but she hadn't been alone. Jinx and Zephyr hadn't been permitted in the closed courtroom. While they hadn't been there, the other victims of Nacin's misdeeds had. Twenty-seven women had testified against him, recalling their interactions with the man and the way he'd mistreated them.

Zephyr and Jinx waited for her in the side hallway. Zephyr rushed up to her first. "Come on." He guided her through the inner workings of the building with Jinx right on their heels.

She didn't mind being whisked away from the cameras. Once she'd publicly accused Nacin, she'd had to face the throng of reporters demanding her statement. Her lawyers had handled the media, but still. One of the biggest gets was her leaving the courtroom.

She'd expected Jinx and Zephyr would have connections to help her leave unseen. She'd ridden with them to and from the courthouse up to now. Like they'd been able to bribe the media to leave her alone. How long was that going to last? And how were they going to get to the car without being seen now that the trial was over?

The verdict rang in her ears. "Guilty." The nightmare wasn't over, though. Nacin had been found guilty of abusing, raping and assaulting his victims, but he hadn't heard his sentence for his misdeeds. She'd go to the sentencing, needing to hear how he'd be punished. But that was for another day.

"This way." Jinx directed them through a set of doors to an elevator. "This is the direct route to the private garage."

"You finally got access?" she asked. She allowed them to tug her into the drafty space. She rushed behind Zephyr to the car and hurried into the backseat. She'd grown accustomed to resting her head on Jinx's lap while Zephyr drove.

"You don't need to hide." Jinx shook his head. "We're not getting out of here without being seen. This just gives us time to get moving without the crush of media against the car."

"What he's trying to say is it's saving the paint." Zephyr backed out of the parking spot. "The shitty part is we're three floors under the building and we still have to come out through the tunnel, which is swarmed with media."

"What do I do?" She'd been hounded by the media to give her side of the story. Despite the offers of money and exclusivity, she refused to give any interviews. The only people who needed to hear what she had to say were in the courtroom. Her pain wasn't for public consumption.

She'd had to live through the scrutiny of the death of Keifer. She'd been blamed for his death and questioned as if she'd been the one to do the deed. The hypocrisy of the situation wasn't lost on her. He'd shot her first, she'd passed out, yet she was blamed for his death. She gritted her teeth. Once the truth came out, once everyone knew how much money Keifer had gambled away, how many personas he'd used and that he'd assaulted others…the public view of her changed.

Disgusting.

Only when it had come to light that Keifer was a bad guy, had she gotten the respect and vindication she deserved. At least he was gone. He'd never hurt her again.

"Ready?" Zephyr asked. "Relax. We'll be through the swarm soon."

Onyx turned her attention to Jinx's phone and forced herself to appear engrossed in whatever he was reading. "I see and you know, it's interesting."

"Isn't it?" he asked, playing along. "And fascinating that it's working. Like they don't know we're not bothering to look up at them."

"Because I don't care what they want from me." She pointed to the photo of a cat on his screen. "Isn't he cute? Why don't we get a cat? I'd love to have a pet."

"You're my pet." He kissed her temple, then swiped to another photo. "Whatever cat you want, that's what you'll get."

"How about one from the shelter? One that's been there a while?" She refused to look up until Zephyr gave her the signal they were in the clear.

"Finally." Jinx darkened his screen. "I hate that shit we have to do until we're out of sight."

She hadn't minded. "I wasn't kidding about wanting a cat." She spent a lot of time at the house alone and would like the company.

"Who said you weren't going to have one?" Jinx asked. "I simply don't like having to pretend we're engrossed in the damn phone. I'd rather be able to drive out of there like everyone else. No big thing."

"Unfortunately, I'm a big thing because I accused a man with more money than God, of something that was atrocious. What's worse, I'm not making a big deal or trying to get my name out there. I'm hiding and that drives the media crazy. It's incomprehensible," she said. "And he was found guilty. You know he'll have his team of lawyers file papers to get the verdict tossed. If there's anything to get him out of trouble, they'll try it."

"Because you made him look stupid," Zephyr said. "At least that's how he sees it. You took his reputation from him."

"He took it from himself. He didn't have permission to do what he did to me." She tensed in Jinx's embrace. "He screwed himself and he's paying for it. Even if it's not going to last and he manages to get the case voided, he still got caught."

"He did." Jinx rubbed her shoulder. "But the jury saw through the bullshit. He tried to lie his way out of it and it didn't work."

"Tried to bully, too." She shoved an errant lock of her hair from her forehead. "Sorry."

"You were through a traumatic situation and it's not over, but it's also not stagnant." Zephyr pulled onto the freeway. "He's got to worry about himself. You don't and from now on tonight, we're not talking about him. We're going to have a good time, enjoy each other and let our troubles go."

She liked the way that sounded. "Okay."

"We're going to play tonight. We'll play, let go and enjoy." Jinx kissed her temple again. "We've got a surprise for you."

"You do?" He had her attention. "What kind of surprise?"

"It's not a kitten. I can't get one of those, not the kind you want, that fast," Jinx said. "But we will."

"You'll like the surprise," Zephyr said. "We've put a lot of work into it."

"Yeah?" She shoved her disdain for the court case aside and embraced her excitement. "I can't wait to find out what it is."

"We had to wait for you to be up to the challenge and surprise," Zephyr said. "And we wanted to get through the legal shit."

"Did you know your ads have brought in a fresh wave of business?" Jinx asked. "We haven't had the chance to tell you, but you bolstered our numbers. People want to talk to the girl who convinced them to have a landscaping team work on their property."

"That's nuts, but I don't want to talk to the public. I'd rather be the face and voice, but not interact." She rubbed her bare arms as a shiver ran the length of her spine. "Do you want more ads?"

"We will, but not yet."

"Oh." She'd been looking forward to working on another campaign. "What did you want to do?"

"Well…" Zephyr pulled into the garage and the room darkened as the door closed. "We thought we'd play."

She hadn't even realized they were home until she sat in the dimly lit space. "Oh." She sat up straighter and realized what they'd requested. "Yes, Sirs."

"Do you want to play?" Jinx asked. "Tell me your safe word."

"Pumpkin, Sirs, but I don't want to use it." She followed Jinx out of the car and bowed her head as she made her way into the house. She wandered straight to the bedroom, then ripped her clothes off. The faster she could get out of the drab business attire she'd chosen to wear to court, the better. She liked color and vibrancy, not the blacks, navys and tans she'd picked.

She perched on the bed, nude and thrilled. She closed her eyes as she waited for them. With her hands clasped at the small of her back, she sat making no sound.

Jinx walked in first. He removed his necktie, then crawled behind her onto the bed. He slid the silk around her face, obscuring her vision. He brushed his hands down her bare shoulders.

She shivered. "Thank you, Sir." She loved having her sight restricted. It heightened her other senses. He trailed his fingertips over her arms, then across the top of her breasts before he pinched her nipple.

Another shiver rocked through her. Something soft rode over her skin and she wanted to look. What was he using? A scarf? No, this was lighter. The end of a crop? This felt different.

He parted her knees and the softness moved over her inner thighs. Her pussy thrummed. Excitement washed through her.

She knew the moment Zephyr walked into the room because his cologne curled around her.

"That's beautiful," Zephyr said. "I love seeing you so free."

She felt the bed move and the springs creak. She leaned into Zephyr's touch, wanting more of him.

"Not yet." He kissed her. "Just a moment."

"Yes, Sirs." She wished she had more patience. She loved being touched. The way they plucked at her nipples, parted her legs, spanked her, made her fly. "Thank you, Sirs."

"Haven't done much yet." Jinx cupped her chin. "Lean forward."

She did as she was told. The scent of him wrapped around her. She opened her mouth and allowed him to fill her to the brim. His curls tickled her nose. She wanted to thank him, but it was impossible. Instead, she bobbed her head, taking him to the back of her throat, then backing nearly all the way from him. He met her movement for movement, building into a steady rhythm with her.

She lost herself in the pleasure of sucking his dick. She loved pleasing him. Loved getting caught up in the thrill of the act. Her pussy creamed. She longed to ease one hand between her legs and caress her clit.

Instead, she focused on him.

"Yes." Jinx petted her head. "I love this." He pumped harder, shoving his cock deeper into her mouth.

"I want in on that," Zephyr said. "Don't keep her only for yourself."

She wanted to be shared.

"Yes." Jinx stopped, then eased the blindfold from her eyes.

She blinked in the rush of bright light. "Sirs?"

"Up." Jinx helped her to her feet, then directed her to bend over with her ass pointed toward him. He grasped her hips. Before she could think or realize what was happening, he plunged into her. He filled her pussy to the hilt.

She gasped. "Thank you, Sirs." She reached for the bed for stability, but Zephyr stepped in front of her.

"Not so easy, bad girl." He unzipped his trousers and shoved the cotton down his thighs. His cock bobbed free from his pants and boxer briefs. She licked her lips. "You know what to do," Zephyr said. "You know how to please yourself."

She paused for a split-second. He hadn't said pleasing him, but *herself*. He knew her too well. She opened her mouth, accepting Zephyr's dick. As one man moved forward, the other retreated enough to create another perfect rhythm.

Her thoughts turned to mush. The moment delighted and spurred her on. She held onto Zephyr's thighs. The harder they moved, the more she loved the treatment.

Just as she grew accustomed to their movements, Jinx and Zephyr both stopped. She brushed her hair from her eyes. Had she done something wrong?

"I need to be inside you." Zephyr took his place behind her and Jinx stood where Zephyr had vacated.

"Do you want us both?" Jinx asked and cupped her chin.

"I do." She said nothing else as she leaned forward and accepted him again. She buried her nose in his curls once more.

At the same time, Zephyr plunged into her cunt, ripping the breath from her.

She swore her head spun. She groaned around Jinx's shaft. The orgasm built within her, starting in her belly, then radiating to her limbs before centering in her pussy. She rocked her hips, trying to get closer to Zephyr.

No matter how hard she tried, she couldn't breathe. Couldn't think. She needed to come.

"Fuck, I need more." Zephyr increased the speed of his movements. He pushed harder into her. "Can't hold back."

"I need…" Jinx rammed into her. "Fuck me." He threaded his fingers into her hair, holding onto her head.

"Come with us." Zephyr slapped her ass. "Come for us." He surged into her hard, his cock vibrating as he cried out and came.

Jinx shuddered and tugged harder on her hair. He pushed to the hilt. His salty cum shot down her throat.

She lapped at him, not wanting to miss anything. While she cleaned him and rode Zephyr's dick, she embraced the orgasm. Her knees weakened. She grasped Jinx's thighs. A whimper escaped her lips and she panted around him.

They'd used her up, filled her and she'd loved every second.

Jinx added a couple more thrusts, then stilled. He withdrew, then knelt in front of her. He kissed her, resting his forehead on hers.

Zephyr held tight to her hips a bit longer before he pulled out. He guided her onto the bed. "Stretch out."

She wasn't going to argue. She stretched and snuggled into the sheets.

Jinx joined her and a moment later, Zephyr crawled along her other side.

"You said you had a surprise," she managed. "This was a great surprise. Thank you, Sirs. I loved it."

"This wasn't the surprise," Jinx said. "That's still to come."

"Oh?" She'd never get enough of them. She'd been through hell and come back, while having them beside her. How could she ever repay them? She'd have to keep proving her love. "Thank you for making me fly."

"It went too fast," Zephyr said. "But I'm glad."

"But this is your surprise." Jinx reached over to the side table and rolled back over with a piece of paper in hand. "This…"

"What is it?" she asked.

Zephyr tugged a blanket over them before he helped unfold the paper. "We don't want you just as our plaything or our employee. We've fallen in love with you, Onyx. The second we saw you at the club, we knew you were special and we're ready to make it official. This contract, a fluid document at the moment, is our way of proving our devotion and desire for you."

She couldn't believe her luck. *A contract?* She gasped as she read the words on the paper. They'd taken into consideration her concerns, her hard nos, her desires and her past.

"Read it and give it time to marinate," Jinx said. "We vow to give you love, devotion and the truth. You're our girl and we endeavor to please, respect and cherish you."

"You're our sub, but you're also in control. You have the right to stop the scene if it's gone too far and it's expected you will tell us when you need a break. We expect you to be honest with us, to give us the chance to hold your heart and show you just how important you are to us," Zephyr said. "Give it time."

"I don't need to." She waggled her fingers. "I'll sign it right now."

"Slow down and make sure you agree to the terms. We've gone to the trouble of making it sexy, fair and respectful," Zephyr said. "You have input."

"Yes, Sirs." She should read it thoroughly, but she trusted them just the same.

"While you read, there's another part of the surprise," Jinx said. "Here."

"It's too much." She shook her head. "You've done too much."

"It's never too much." Zephyr produced a small flocked box. "Jinx and I worked on the design, he created it and we had the jeweler make these to our standards. There are three rings, all matching, to show that we're all intertwined."

"It's a symbol of our union," Jinx added.

She stared at the rings. Three bands decorated with knots. "They're intricate and delicate." The knots were beautiful and complicated. "I'm impressed."

"Just impressed?" Zephyr asked. "We worked hard on those."

Jinx propped himself on his elbow. "We wanted to create something you could wear all the time that wasn't a collar, but still showed our connection."

"They do and I love them." She couldn't wait to wear hers. They kept acting so fearful. That she'd reject them? Not at all. She was honored to be their girl and thrilled to have been chosen.

"These are the ones for everyday wear, but we couldn't give you only this one." Zephyr slid the ring onto her left hand. "You deserve something as beautiful as you."

"And this isn't?" She admired the ring. The silver glinted in the light.

Zephyr opened the bottom of the flocked box. The new flap moved out of the way, revealing another ring. The blood-red gemstone glittered in the bright silver setting. Diamond sparkled around the stone in a delicate frame. "You're our gem."

"Precious stones and metal for a precious person," Jinx said. "The best gems and pure platinum."

"Oh my God." She couldn't believe it. "For me?" She didn't deserve this.

"For you." Zephyr grasped her left hand. "Will you accept our contract and our hearts?"

"Accept us as your Sirs, but also your lovers and partners?" Jinx asked. "We can't imagine this life without you."

Tears filled her eyes. She tried to speak, but the words wouldn't come. She summoned her strength. This was too important of a moment to mess up. "Of course I will. I love it. Love all of it. I can't wait to start this next chapter of my life because I get to start it with you."

"I love you, Onyx," Jinx said. "You have my heart."

"I love you, too, sweetheart. You're the part we've been missing and can't lose," Zephyr said. "We truly believe it. You're our gem."

How could she turn down sincerity and devotion like this? Easy. She couldn't. "I love you both. You, Jinx, are the sweet, artsy, silly man I've been looking for." She turned to Zephyr. "You're the tense, determined, focused man I never knew I needed, but can't live without. You both make me happy and give me freedom I never knew was possible." They'd been able to protect her from a lifetime of being destroyed by

Nacin. They'd saved her from Keifer. Saved her from a life of dread and pain. They'd given her the chance to fly. To regain her strength. To have the life she deserved. To be herself.

"We have time to sort this all out, but as long as we know you're staying, then no amount of time is too great." Zephyr kissed her. "Our love."

"You're my loves, too." She kissed him back, then kissed Jinx. "You made me believe in my worth and showed me just how wonderful life can be. I want to be with you. Forever."

"Good." Jinx tucked to her side. "You're not just another sweet smile in an advertisement. You're our girl. Our love."

She'd never heard sweeter words in her life. Now she had time to figure out her life with her men beside her. Not too bad for a woman who'd believed her place was in front of a camera, doing nothing but posing and smiling.

She finally belonged.

Sign up for our newsletter and find out about all our romance book releases, eBook sales and promotions, sneak peeks and FREE romance books!

Want to see more from this author? Here's a taster for you to enjoy!

Christmas in North Bend
Wendi Zwaduk

Excerpt

Alex West stood in the middle of the concourse at Cleveland Hopkins airport and toyed with the handle of his bag. His assistant, Jill Gosk, fiddled with her phone and growled. The people on the plane had been irritated by the lateness of the flight and the snow delaying their landing a few minutes. He didn't mind. Christmas, even seven days away, was the time to slow down and spend precious hours with family and friends—not stress over things he couldn't control.

"What's the matter?" He noticed a dusting of snow on the windowsill and wished he were out in the cold. He loved Christmas in Ohio, even if he hadn't spent much time in the state in a few years. "Jill?"

"The car should be ready so all we have to do is retrieve your bags from the claims area. According to my app, the bags are down there." Jill glanced about. "This is a tiny airport."

"It's not LAX, but it works." He pointed to the corridor. "Let's get the luggage." He nudged her forward. "I don't know what I'd do without you. Girl, you save my butt almost every day." He grinned and fell into step beside her. "How's Nick?"

She blushed. "I—I didn't think you knew about him."

"He called to tell me you were together," Alex said. "I told him I was happy for you. I'm glad you found each other." He rode the escalator to the ground floor. The sound of Christmas carols echoed in the air, along with the din of conversation. He watched the people moving about. There were stories in these folks. Stories about love lost, love found, people reconnecting and the joy of Christmas. He chuckled to himself. He could use these bits and pieces for his own upcoming writing. The book wouldn't write itself and he needed the right push to get started.

"Here. Our bags are in carousel C." Jill marched up to the revolving belt filled with luggage. "Keep your eyes peeled."

"Sure will." Alex sighed. He trusted Jill with his schedule and his business dealings. She knew how to get him from point A to point B without issue. He slid his gaze over the array of bags. "Either I'm wrong, or I don't see mine." He pointed to her lavender suitcase. "There's yours."

She nodded and grabbed her bags from the belt. "Got them. Yours should be along." She checked her phone again and turned the screen around. "See? The app says they're here."

"Right, but they're on the second time through and mine aren't there. I've kept an eye out." He glanced over her shoulder at the phone. "The app is wrong."

"It can't be." She massaged her temple. "They have to be here."

He'd learned not to let minor setbacks get to him. Being a writer meant having a thick skin. Just because one person didn't like his work didn't mean a myriad of others agreed. Besides, who could be upset at Christmas? "It's okay. We'll go to the lost luggage department." He guided her and her bag away from the carousel. "My bags are probably halfway to Chicago."

"I'm so sorry, RR."

She'd used his pen name. He shouldn't be annoyed, but he'd rather be referred to by his given name in this instance. "Don't sweat it. We're on the way to my parents and I'm sure I can borrow some of my father's clothes until my luggage gets here — if we didn't simply go to the wrong carousel." He'd bet the bags were on the wrong plane, but he saw no reason to get upset. "It's going to be all right." He strode up to the counter.

The woman at the desk smiled, but before he could speak, Jill stepped forward.

"Hi. I booked the flight for Mr. Taylor and we've arrived, but his luggage hasn't. I have the information on the app and everything." Jill held up her phone. "See?"

The woman smiled again. "Let me check your information." She paused. "RR Taylor? As in the author RR Taylor?"

"That's me." He offered his hand. "I'm heading over to North Bend for Christmas with my family and to do a book signing the day after tomorrow. If you're available, you should stop in."

"I'm working all week," the attendant said. "But it's great to meet you. I've read all your books. I loved *Crispin in New York*."

"Thank you. If you have a piece of paper, I'll autograph it for you." He waited for her to give him something to write on, then signed the page with a special note for her. "There. Enjoy."

"Thank you." The attendant beamed. "Wow." She tucked the paper into her front pocket. "I wish I had better news for you concerning your bags. According to my tracking system, your luggage was rerouted to

New York and will be back in two days. We can call you when it's at the terminal."

"No," Jill said. "He needs his clothes."

"I'll get by." He placed his hand on Jill's arm and turned his attention to the attendant. "Thank you. Where can I leave my information?" Not having his clothes or the presents he'd brought for his family wasn't ideal, but he had little choice.

"I've got it on file with your baggage and flight numbers," the attendant said. "I'll be in touch."

"Thank you. I hope I have my luggage before Christmas. If I don't, then I don't. I hope you have a Merry Christmas, too." He nudged Jill. "We should go."

"I messed up," Jill said. "This is bad."

"You didn't mess up." He nodded to the sign directing them to the car rental counter. "Why don't you check on the car?"

"Oh yeah." She darted away with her phone.

Alex sighed. Jill was a sweet woman, but so highly strung. He thanked the cosmos she'd come into his orbit to help with his promotional needs, but he could use a break from her. He followed behind her, but at a bit of a distance. One of his plans wasn't going so well. Time to check on another of his schemes. He sent a text to Nick.

Are you at the hotel? She's upset about my luggage being lost. Might need to be extra sweet to her. Do you have everything you need for tonight?

Alex didn't wait for a response and instead tucked his phone into his jacket pocket. He hurried after Jill. He'd worked with her boyfriend to facilitate Nick's proposal that night. Jill would be happy, Nick would have the woman he loved and Alex would have a break.

Jill stopped walking and her shoulders slumped. Her brow crinkled. She still had her phone to her ear. "You don't understand. I reserved the car a month ago. We need that vehicle. I don't care if it's the holidays. We have places to be. No, I don't want…my client is leaving. Hold on." She stopped Alex. "Wait."

"Take a breath. It's Christmas. Everyone is on the edge and you getting upset isn't helping. The more you and I flip out, the more upset everyone else will be." He pointed to the rental counter. "Let's check on the car in person."

"I'll handle it." Jill pushed past him. "Wait over there."

He should argue with her, but he'd just given his speech on being calm. Disputing wouldn't get him anywhere. Part of him didn't mind taking his time while getting to North Bend, but the rest of him wanted to unite Jill with Nick. Then she'd relax. Good thing Alex had flown Nick in ahead of time and had him installed in the hotel in North Bend.

Alex waited by the bank of windows and stared out at the planes on the tarmac. His thoughts wandered. Why had he stayed away from North Bend for so long? He loved the snow and quiet of Ohio and appreciated the small-town feel of his home base, but his apartment in Los Angeles had everything he needed. His favorite restaurants were within walking distance and while he didn't want for anything entertainment-wise, he missed his friends in North Bend. The people he'd grown up and come of age with. He had so many fond memories of the town. Plus…there was Molly.

He held his bag tighter. Before he'd left town, he had to see Molly. They'd been so tight. He'd once thought he'd marry her. He'd never forget the blue of her eyes, the softness of her hair or the way she blushed when she smiled. They'd been the best of friends and she'd been his first girlfriend. *First lots of things.* Then they'd gone their separate ways. When they'd been together, he'd told her everything. She'd confided in him when she'd flunked her driving test and when she'd thought he wanted to fix her up with their mutual friend Tony. She hadn't been in love with Tony — she'd loved Alex.

Flashes of his years with Molly came to mind — volunteering at the Santa Barn, secret Santa shopping and all those visits to the library... He'd heard about her opening the bookstore and vowed he'd sign books at the shop.

Wouldn't she be surprised when she saw him? Was she single? He'd forgotten to ask his mother about Molly's relationship status when he'd planned his trip back to Ohio. But wouldn't his mother have mentioned Molly being married? Wouldn't Molly have invited him to the wedding — if she'd gotten hitched?

Jill stomped up to him. "Okay. So, here's the problem. We must have a car, but we can't have two like I wanted. Just one, so we have to share."

"I thought that was the plan." It had been when he'd canceled her vehicle. She didn't need a separate car if Nick had one and they'd be together.

"This isn't right. Your luggage is missing, we've only got one car... What else can go wrong?" Jill asked.

"The luggage will come back and the car situation is fine."

"Oh no." Jill pinched the bridge of her nose. "It's snowing."

"I've driven in snow."

"It's cold."

"Ohio is cold," Alex said. He stared at her. "You're holding something back. What's the rest of the issue?"

"I miss Nick. It's Christmas and I'm not with the one I love." She sighed. "I need some sleep and a few hours to regroup. I hate being this grouchy."

"You're stressed. It happens." He grasped her shoulder. "Don't worry about it. You never know — Nick might be waiting at the hotel."

"Fat chance." She sank onto the closest chair. "You don't understand. I'm being pouty, and I hate it. The thing is, I thought I could do this job, but I feel like I'm failing. I'm sorry."

"Stress is a pain in the neck." He sat beside her and took the keys from her. "Take a few moments to recover. While I'm driving us to North Bend, why don't you call Nick? That'll make you feel better."

"Ugh. That's the other part of this. I tried to call him, but I can't get an answer."

He checked his phone. The LED light flashed green, meaning he had a new text. He retrieved the message from Nick.

Here and ready for the surprise. I can't wait.

Good. Nick was in place. Alex tucked his phone in his pocket again. "Well, why not try again? He might have been temporarily engaged." *Drat.* He should've chosen a different word. "Just call him."

Jill stared at him. "How can you be so calm? Is it because you're going to see Molly over Christmas?"

"Maybe." *Not really.* Thinking about seeing his friend excited him. He hasn't spent time with her in forever. He missed their friendship. Plus, he wanted to know why they'd drifted apart.

"Well, she seems nice." Jill stood. "I feel better. Thanks for letting me freak out."

He joined her and started toward the doors leading to the row of rental cars. "You're welcome."

"How long is the drive to North Bend?" She fell into step beside him. "It's far away from here, isn't it?"

"About an hour and a half." He stopped at the parking slot containing the SUV. "This is what we have?"

"The dark blue behemoth. It was the only one not rented out." Jill tried the passenger-side door. "It's not the compact one, but it'll do."

"See? That's the Christmas spirit." He climbed behind the wheel of the SUV. "Here's to the next leg of our journey. You'll have plenty of room to stretch out and it would appear there's satellite radio, so your favorite channels are on here, too."

"Something is finally normal," Jill said. "Yes."

"As for you doing your job, don't worry. I wouldn't be in Ohio without you." He could, but she needed the reassurance. "It's Christmas. We start being jolly as of right now. We won't let work get us upset and won't worry about the signing. The spirit of the season is around us and we're going to have fun." If he had his way, Jill and Nick would be engaged that night and he'd have the next book started. Merry Christmas.

* * * *

Two hours later, Alex drove past the North Bend city limits sign. He rolled down the main drag. The town now had three gas stations instead of one, the hotel had grown—which he'd learned when he'd helped Nick book the suite—and there was now a big box store just over the city line. Still, North Bend had a small-town feel. Every business in town was either on Main Street or Church Street—crisscrossing at the center of town. Tinsel and lights decorated each lamp post, an inflatable Santa and thirty-foot pine tree towered in the town square and a row of evergreen trees stood sentry duty in front of the hardware store. Every pole and sign featured lights and garland. He'd forgotten just how pretty the town could be—like a Christmas card come to life.

Alex sighed. The Christmas spirit he'd longed for swirled around him. He parked in front of the hotel under the awning.

"Why are we here?" Jill asked. "We're staying with your parents, aren't we?" She paused. "Aren't we?"

"You're staying here. I thought you might want a break from me and deserved some pampering. I've made all the arrangements for you to be here while I'm at my parents' house." He shifted in his seat. "You work hard. Consider this my Christmas present to you." Nick had a lot to do with her being there, but Alex wasn't about to let her know that yet. The surprise was Nick's to disclose.

"How will I get around?"

Drat. He had to think of something quick. Something besides Nick had a car for them to use. "I'll stop by my parents' house and borrow one of their vehicles to get around. I'll drop this one off here and use that one."

"Don't you need me close?" she asked.

"It's Christmas and this is one signing. I can fly solo for a while."

"You've mentioned the Christmas thing," Jill said.

"Enjoy this gift. You don't have to deal with me for a while. Isn't that worth something?" He sure hoped Nick was in the lobby waiting for her.

"You did this all by yourself? You never make plans."

"I let you set up the signing schedule, but I can handle going out on my own. I've done it before—I used to control my entire schedule before you came along." He nodded to the door. "Go. I'm a call away if you need me." If the plans were still in place, she'd get her Christmas wish of engagement to Nick, and Alex would have time to explore North Bend.

"I'm not wild about this plan, but I'll go. Call me if you need anything." She left the car, then, with his help, retrieved her bags from the rear of the SUV.

"You'll have a good time," Alex said. "Promise."

"I'll be at the signing. I won't miss it," Jill said.

"I know, and I appreciate your diligence. I've got this." He hugged her, then waved. "Merry Christmas."

"I'll see you before Christmas," she muttered. She stole glances at him as she made her way into the hotel.

Nick stood in the lobby and held roses. If Alex wasn't mistaken, he heard Jill shriek. He watched her embrace Nick. Alex tended to strike out in love, but he appreciated seeing two people fall for each other. Molly had once told him he loved love. Maybe. If nothing else, he'd helped make Nick and Jill's Christmas desire come true.

He left his post beside the vehicle and slid into the driver's seat. He drummed on the steering wheel. Christmas, as well as love, was a strange thing. Some people weren't thrilled by the change of season and chill in the air. Some fell into depression. Others found excitement and fulfillment in the electricity in the air. He embraced the joy of Christmas.

He pulled away from the hotel and started down Main Street. Alex stopped at the traffic light and noticed the bookstore. He'd seen the images of the store on the webpage, but the real view was better. Books arranged as letters served as the signage for the establishment. Christmas lights ringed each window and a Christmas tree hulked on the sidewalk in front.

Alex would bet Molly had the shelves packed with great books. Part of him wanted to visit and check out the place, but the rest of him refrained. He'd be there tomorrow. The signing wasn't for another day and a half. Right now, he needed to get to his parents' house.

He drove through the housing development on the east end of town on the way to his childhood home. There were Christmas lights everywhere. All the area needed now was fresh snow. He almost wanted to break out in a carol or two.

He parked in his parents' driveway, then schlepped his carry-on bag into the house. Despite the lights and decorations on every conceivable surface of the home, the place wasn't the same. No chaos, no people...and no dog. Without those, he felt lost. He couldn't chastise his parents on their lack of a dog—he didn't have one either. He wanted one. He needed a companion.

Alex sank onto one of the stools at the bar. How could a guy with a great life and what he'd always wanted for a career consider changing most of it after one night back in his home town? Because he'd never gotten North Bend out of his system or forgotten Molly. Because his carefully crafted life wasn't as bright as he wanted everyone to think and he didn't have any words for the next book. He hated writer's block, but he couldn't concentrate.

The night he'd broken things off with Molly came to mind. She hadn't argued with him when he'd said he'd call her later. *Famous last words...* He'd broken up with her to follow his dream. He'd thought he was doing the best for them both, but he'd been a jerk. Now he'd come back and wanted her to be nice to him? *Huh. She should tell me to get lost.*

He paused. The house was too silent. Where was everyone? He fiddled with his phone and called his mother. Maybe she'd give him a better idea of what to do and where the heck she and his father were. After two rings, she answered.

"Hi sweetheart. You're home? Already?" she asked.

"I'm at the house. You went a little berserk with the lights and garland, didn't you? I don't remember this much glitter when I was a kid," he said. "It's like walking into a gingerbread house."

"Oh, it's just a few things," she said and laughed. "Did you bring a girlfriend with you? There's food in the fridge and plenty of wood in the bin. We anticipated you'd be hungry."

"Thanks. I appreciate you thinking of me." He sounded so formal. This was his mother. He didn't have to walk on pins and needles with her. "I'm on my own—no girlfriend—so there's more than enough to eat." He pinched the bridge of his nose. "You don't have to worry about me, Mom."

"It's my job to worry," his mother said. "Have you visited Molly?"

"I'll get there," he said. "Will you be home for the signing?"

"Sure. I know it seems like we forgot about you, but this is the big anniversary. Forty years. Can you imagine being with someone for more than half your life?" She laughed again. "Your father planned a dinner tonight with the Pfafs, then we're off to see the new action movie. I don't know what it's called. We're staying in Erie for one more night, then we'll be home in the morning and at the signing. I won't miss this. My son signing books in my local bookstore. My son, the brilliant author."

Brilliant author? His mother knew how to pump his ego.

Alex left the phone on the bar and glanced over at the fridge. Cooking wasn't his forte. He excelled at burning things and ordering takeout. But he had to eat.

He shrugged out of his sport coat, then crossed the room to the closet. Ages ago, he'd left his leather jacket in there. "Please, Mom, tell me you didn't donate my coat." He opened the door and found the jacket. "Score! Thanks, Mom." He donned the garment and breathed in the scent of the leather.

Life wasn't exactly how he'd planned, but not all that bad, either. The time on the plane and worrying about getting to North Bend had caught up with him. He needed a few hours' sleep. Since he had the house to himself, he might as well catch a few winks. If he was going to win Molly back, he had to be on top form.

About the Author

Wendi Zwaduk is a multi-published, award-winning author of more than one-hundred short stories and novels. She's been writing since 2008 and published since 2009. Her stories range from the contemporary and paranormal to BDSM and LGBTQ themes. No matter what the length, her works are always hot, but with a lot of heart. She enjoys giving her characters a second chance at love, no matter what the form. She's been the runner up in the Kink Category at Love Romances Café as well as nominated at the LRC for best contemporary, best ménage and best anthology. Her books have made it to the bestseller lists on Amazon.com and the former AllRomance Ebooks. She also writes under the name of Megan Slayer.

When she's not writing, she spends time with her husband and son as well as three dogs and three cats. She enjoys art, music and racing, but football is her sport of choice.

Wendi loves to hear from readers. You can find her contact information, website details and author profile page at https://www.firstforromance.com

ENTWINED PUBLISHING